I, GLORIA GOLD

Gloria Gold has sacrificed her entire life for her family – and are they grateful? Not a bit! Her husband Morry, who's in the rag trade, picks at the huge meals she cooks and reads a book rather than talk to her. Her son Robert shows no interest in girls, and daughter Sharon is already thirty-four with no sign of finding a husband or producing some grandchildren. She won't even tell Gloria her address.

What does a 56-year-old Jewish housewife from North London *do* when she's so obviously unappreciated? Gloria decides to spend a little less time fighting domestic germs and write her autobiography instead. When they read it, her selfish family will know just how much they have taken her for granted.

But somehow autobiography proves to be a more difficult art than Gloria had anticipated, despite the help of Christian Foggart, the handsome teacher of her evening class in creative writing. For whenever she sets out to explore the past, she finds it impossible to tell the unvarnished truth, and the present intrudes on her thoughts in an ever more alarming way.

In this original, hilariously funny novel, Judith Summers tells the story of an ordinary housewife whose traditional way of life and aspirations for the future are being challenged every day by the liberated, 1980s values of her children. Despite her terrible fears and prejudices, we end up laughing with Gloria rather than at her as she struggles to learn some tolerance for other people's lifestyles. At once witty and naïve, warm-hearted and exasperating, Gloria Gold takes us with her on an exhilarating voyage of self-discovery that leads to unexpected love.

By the same author

DEAR SISTER

I, GLORIA GOLD

Judith Summers

COLLINS
8 Grafton Street, London W1
1988

William Collins Sons & Co. Ltd
London · Glasgow · Sydney · Auckland
Toronto · Johannesburg

Note

This is a work of fiction. All the characters who
appear in this novel are wholly imaginary and are not
intended to bear any resemblance to any real person,
living or dead.

First published 1988
Copyright © Judith Summers 1988

BRITISH LIBRARY CATALOGUING IN PUBLICATION DATA

Summers, Judith
I, Gloria Gold.
I. Title
823'.914[F]   PR6069.U3/

ISBN 0-00-223314-2

Photoset in Linotron Galliard by
Rowland Phototypesetting Ltd
Bury St Edmunds, Suffolk
Printed in Great Britain by
Robert Hartnoll (1985) Ltd, Bodmin

For Honey and David

Prologue

I, Gloria Gold, an ordinary Jewish housewife, have decided to write my autobiography.

I made up my mind to embark on this venture last week, while I was shampooing the hall carpet in the middle of the night. As any housewife knows, performing this task during the day is a complete waste of time: no sooner have you reached the kitchen than someone rings the front bell, and you are forced to walk back over the freshly-washed part in order to answer it; or if you start at the kitchen you end up at the front door remembering that you've left something boiling on the stove. Either way, your work is ruined, for there are clearly detectable footprints all over the damp pile. Once, when the front bell rang at lunchtime and I was stranded in the middle of the hall, I made the mistake of popping out the back door to see who was there. Imagine my horror when it slammed shut behind me! I was locked out in the rain without keys, coat or handbag, and I had to go to a neighbour's house to telephone my wonderful husband Morry, who was far from pleased to be taken away from his work.

'For God's sake, Gloria,' he shouted as the car pulled

up outside and he hurled his keys from the window. 'It's only a carpet. You're meant to walk on it!' 'I know you are,' I shouted back from the porch. 'But not until the druggets have gone down!'

I am extremely protective of my pale-beige hall carpet. I am proud to say that although it was laid seven years ago, it still looks as good as new. 'But no one can see it!' my darling daughter Sharon said when I first covered it with druggets. 'Who cares?' I said firmly. 'As long as they know it's there.'

What does Sharon know about such things? Though a beautiful girl and a successful television producer, she has never cleaned a carpet in her life, and probably has no idea how to use a Hoover. I doubt she even sweeps the kitchen floor in her flat in Kentish Town. What right has she got to criticize my druggets? After all, they are practical, just like polythene dust covers, which can be wiped clean in a jiffy with a damp cloth and a little diluted household cleanser. What is the point of spending hundreds of pounds on pale-peach Dralon upholstery if it gets ruined in a week? 'What's the point of spending any money if you never sit on what you pay for?' Morry frequently says when he's in the living-room. 'You are sitting on it, Morry,' I tell him. 'No I'm not,' he says. 'I'm sitting on plastic.'

When he says these things my eyes fill with tears. 'Don't you want a home that's fit to live in?' I ask him. 'Don't I keep the place clean and tidy for you?'

Dear Morry! Such a wonderful husband! How shall I describe him? He is a good head taller than I am, which is five feet four, though since he has gone bald on top he seems a little shorter. He has brown eyes and cheeks the colour of poached salmon, and although his face looks quite thin under those horn-rimmed reading glasses, he has a nice pot-belly to show the world that I feed him well. In character he is kindness personified. Even though he sometimes shouts at me about the high standards of hygiene I insist on, I know in my heart-of-hearts that he doesn't mean a word he says.

I do not consider myself to be fanatical about cleanliness. I simply take my role as wife and mother seriously enough to be concerned about protecting those I love from disease. God knows what germs they could pick up in the street, when any passer-by might be riddled with typhoid, hepatitis, or even worse. As for the kitchens of all those nightclubs my handsome, thirty-year-old son Robert eats out in, they must be crawling with germs. However, I'm glad to say that the kitchen of Robert's flat in Hampstead is spotless. But then Robert, who is an accountant in an advertising agency, is very particular in his ways. Unlike Sharon. As for her kitchen – I can't bear to think about it. Not that I've seen it. Oh no, I haven't been invited, not in five years. Not only that, but she's never told me her address.

'Are you afraid I'll drop in without warning you?' I asked her when she came round to visit us the other day.

'Of course not,' she lied.

'Then what?' I said. She said nothing, but her face closed up like a kitchen cupboard and she wedged herself more tightly in the armchair. 'I ought to know where you live, darling,' I coaxed. 'I mean, what if there's an emergency and I need to get hold of you in a hurry? Say, God forbid, your father had a heart attack in the middle of the night. How would I contact you?'

'You could phone me. You've got the number.'

'What if the phone was out of order?'

She sighed deeply. 'Oh, Mum, for God's sake!'

'Why can't I come and see the flat?' I persisted with uncharacteristic frankness.

She stood up to her full height of five feet seven, ran her fingers through her long unruly brown curls, and walked on her slender gazelle-legs across to the window. 'It's not your kind of place,' she muttered as she stared out into the street. 'You just wouldn't like it.'

Of course I wouldn't like it, and Sharon knows why. It's not only because it's filthy, and because of that cat she insists on keeping, it's because she's living there with a flatmate. A male flatmate. Exactly what kind of mate is he? That's what I'd like to know. And what else does she share with him apart from the flat?

Enough. A mother's life is rewarding but difficult. I no longer have control over what my children do in the outside world. All I can do is ensure that I myself set a good moral example, and that their home – when they deign to come back to it – has a well-stocked fridge and is as hygienic as I can possibly make it. As any housewife knows, this is a daunting, demanding job, a bit like painting the Forth Bridge: no sooner has one completed the task in hand than it needs doing all over again. I'll tell you another good thing about shampooing the carpets after midnight – it saves time. How I will ever manage to write my autobiography when I've so much housework to do, I really don't know.

There I was, in the small hours of the morning last week, going over the dusty patch under the doormat with my electric shampooer. Usually I get a great deal of pleasure from watching the circles of snowy foam break in white waves across the deep pile, but last week . . . Well, last week I found the whole operation strangely unsatisfying. I'm ashamed to say that I was not really concentrating. My mind was elsewhere, worrying about the children. You see, I'm afraid that Robert is . . . that Robert might be . . . And that if he is he might have . . . No, it's too awful, I can't write it down. If I do, Morry might see it. And if I put it into words, I'll have to believe it. As it is, it's only a mother's worry, so I'll try and put it out of my mind.

But as for Sharon, she and I had had another set-to on the phone that night. As usual, she'd accused me of starting it. I certainly did not. All I'd said was that she wasn't getting any younger and wasn't it time she gave up that useless job and concentrated on finding a husband to settle down with. Well, I've never known a person to be so touchy.

'How dare you call my job useless?' she flared down the telephone.

'Of course I dare,' I said. 'I'm your mother.'

'That doesn't give you the right to tell me what to do!'

'I'm not telling you anything, darling. I only made a suggestion.'

'Well,' she said huffily. 'I suggest that you mind your own business in future.'

'I'm your mother, Sharon, so your business is my business. When, please God, you have your own family some day, you'll learn that it's part of the bond between mother and child.'

'You're forgetting that I'm not a child any more. I'm thirty-four.'

Tears came to my eyes. 'Please, don't remind me,' I choked. Thirty-four and still not married! Not even dating seriously as far as I know. It breaks my heart, really it does. Why, all my friends' daughters are married – some of them no older than Sharon have been married and divorced several times. Plain girls, not nearly as pretty as she could be if she made a bit more effort. I ask you, if they can find man after man to marry them, why can't she find one?

'I know you think I'm an interfering old busybody, darling,' I said, trying to calm her down. 'But it's time you came to your senses, and started looking seriously for a husband. After all, you're not getting any younger. If you're not careful you'll wake up one day and find that all the eligible men have already been snapped up. You'll have to settle for second-best then, and it might even be too late to . . . too late to . . .' I stopped.

'Too late to what?' she said, her anger simmering like water in a pot.

'Nothing, dear.'

The water bubbled impatiently. 'Go on, say it.'

'No, no, it was nothing.'

'Say it!'

I took a deep breath. 'Well, by then it might be too late for you to have children.'

She must have been anticipating my answer, because her top blew even before my last words were out. 'For God's sake, Mum! Not this again! Don't you ever think of anything but grandchildren?'

'I have no grandchildren to think about,' I said. 'I'm only thinking of you.'

'Have you ever thought that I might not want to have children at the moment?'

'When do you propose to have them? When you're sixty-four?'

'Or that I might not want them at all?'

I laughed. 'Don't be absurd, Sharon, every woman wants children.'

'On what evidence do you base that?' she said.

Not for the first time since she graduated from university, I cursed myself for ever having allowed her to study

Sociology. She is always arguing with facts and figures. 'On the evidence of my own eyes,' I said. 'On my own experience. Wanting to have children is only natural.'

'Not necessarily. Many of the women I know don't feel the need for them.'

That doesn't surprise me at all. I mean, what kind of women does Sharon know? Career women who never give a thought to anyone but themselves, that's who. 'In my day,' I continued, 'there was none of this business about "feeling the need". We just got pregnant and that was that.'

'Well,' she countered. 'Isn't it better now that people can choose?'

'I suppose so,' I said doubtfully. 'Frankly, Sharon, sometimes I'm not sure. What if they all chose not to? The human race would come to an end, wouldn't it? And then where would we be?'

She gave a deep sigh. 'How did this stupid conversation start?'

'I think it's a very important conversation. We were discussing your marriage plans.'

'I don't have any,' she said in a strained voice.

'Then you should make some. Join a few synagogue committees so you meet the right kind of person . . .'

'I don't have time.'

'You'd have plenty of time if you gave up that job. Remember, darling, a career isn't everything. Why, marriage fulfils a woman. And a wife has position. She is revered and respected!'

'I have all the respect I need from my colleagues,' she said in a curt voice.

It was then that the desperation I often feel when I talk to her set in. 'Listen to me, Sharon,' I pleaded. 'I'm only saying this because I'm seriously worried about you.'

'Well, I wish you'd stop, Mum,' she said. My heart leapt: was I imagining it, or was there something like real concern in her voice? 'I'm all right,' she continued. 'Really I am. In fact, I'm very happy at the moment.'

'How can a girl of your age be happy on her own?' I said suspiciously.

'I'm not on my own,' she said.

'Oh?'

'I mean,' she went on quickly, 'I've got lots of friends. And there's my cat. And I've got a terrific, exciting, well-paid job which I love.'

Friends, a cat and a job! These are the things that make her happy? 'Well, you needn't give your job up for ever,' I said. 'You can always go back to it when your children are grown up.'

'Television's not like that. One can't just opt out and in again as one wishes. One has to be committed to it.'

'Your father is committed to his business. But he still finds time for a social life.'

'And so do I.'

'Well, I don't see any evidence of it.'

The next time she spoke her voice had become cold again. 'Look, Mum, can't you just take it on trust that I'm fine?' And when I started to protest that she wasn't, she cut me short. 'Frankly, I think you're the unhappy one,' she said.

'Me?' I gasped.

'Yes, you, Mum,' she said. 'You don't know what to do with yourself since Robert and I left home.'

Was that a speck of grime on the telephone seat? I scraped it off with a fingernail. 'I've never heard such rubbish,' I said. 'Why, you both moved out years ago. What do you think I've been doing all the time since, twiddling my thumbs? There's your father to look after and the cooking to do and –'

'There's more to life than making meat loaf,' she interrupted. 'No wonder you're bored.'

'I am not bored!'

'It's not surprising that you sit there worrying about us all the time,' she sighed. 'You've nothing else to think about. What you need is something to do, something that will fulfil you as a person.'

'I am fulfilled, thank you very much,' I snapped. 'And for your information I never stop doing.'

'I'm not talking about housework,' she said. 'There are other things in life. I mean, you're stuck in that house day after day, week in, week out. Don't you think it's time you developed some outside interests?'

'Like what?'

'A hobby or something,' she suggested brightly. 'Gardening, for instance.'

I laughed. 'Get filthy soil under my fingernails? You must be out of your mind.'

'Politics, then.'

'What do you suggest, that I should become Prime Minister?'

'You could always learn Cordon Bleu cookery.'

'Aren't my roast chickens good enough for you any more? Any other bright ideas?'

'Oh, for God's sake! Surely you don't need me to tell you what to do. I mean, there's a whole world out there waiting to be explored –'

'So now you want me to be an explorer!'

She sighed again – a patronizing, impatient kind of sigh. 'Look, Mum, it's your life, so it's up to you. All I'm saying is, it's time you stopped fretting about us and thought about yourself. You're an intelligent woman, you could do anything you wanted to. You could get a job, do charity work or an Open University degree. You could even write a book.'

No wonder I'm worried about Sharon. Don't get me wrong – she's a marvellous girl and I couldn't say a word against her. But what mother wouldn't be worried when they've had to put up with all the things I've had to put up with over the years? And now this! I thought to myself, yanking the plug out of the socket and bringing the shampooer to a wheezing halt at the foot of the stairs. She wants me to write a book! Now she's really gone off her rocker. For if there's anything Sharon knows I hate, it's books.

I am not an uneducated woman. After all, I am Jewish, and we Jews have always been renowned for our learning. And I am well aware that in order to be learned, people must read. But after they've been read, books should be put away in an appropriate place. Because books, while being the depositories of all written knowledge, are also depositories of germs. In our religion we have known this for a long time: don't the Rabbis always lock the Holy Scrolls in the Ark when they've finished with them? But Morry, though a good Jew in many respects, insists on ignoring the Rabbis' example when it comes to this one thing. It is no wonder that books have become a bone of contention between us.

I do not object to his having them, only to the fact that he leaves them lying around when he is not reading them. If I'm not careful there are books everywhere – stacked up on the bedside table and the lavatory floor, and heaped in untidy piles on the living-room coffee-table. It has become a ritual part of our marriage for me to gather them all up when Morry has gone to work in the morning and to put them away where they belong: in the cupboard under the stairs. When Morry comes home at night, he eats his supper without even missing them. But half-way through the evening, usually while I am washing up the supper dishes, he yells from the living-room, 'Where are they?' to which I yell back, 'Which one?' 'All of them, Gloria.' 'All?' I say. 'Morry, you've only got one pair of eyes!'

Believe me, I love my husband dearly. Naturally I do – I have been married to him for thirty-six years. Truly, I couldn't say a word against him. Like my sister Ruth, he runs a wholesale dress business in London's West End, making skirts and blouses to sell to the Oxford Street stores, and, though not a rich man, he has always been a good provider. He is kind, thoughtful, and unusually placid by temperament. Yet despite all these qualities, I sometimes think this mania of his for reading will drive me mad. Even at breakfast his nose is buried in the *Daily Telegraph*, a nasty, sooty paper as far as I'm concerned that leaves grime on his hands and completely ruins the sheets if he reads it in bed. When he comes home in the evening it is always with an evening paper tucked under his arm. After giving me a quick peck on the cheek, he sinks on to the sofa to consult the shares index. He usually finishes the crossword over our evening meal, and then loses himself in a novel or two while watching television. Any attempts I make to engage him in interesting conversation and thus wean him off the written word always fail miserably.

Surely it's unnatural for a man to read so much and talk so little? It can't be good for him. That it's unhealthy for everyone else in the house, I'm certain. Why, the very objects themselves are a hazard. You have to be in a constant state of red-alert when you walk around our house or a book will leap out in front of you and trip you up.

By the time I'd finished cleaning the carpet on that fateful night last week, my mind was fully occupied with worrying about Sharon. As I trudged up to bed in my slippers, so worried was I that I failed to notice the death-trap lurking on the top-but-one stair. It caught my foot and sent me sprawling forward. My first thought as I lay face down on the landing was, Good God, Morry's trying to murder me. My second thought was, I'm going to murder Morry instead. I picked the bloody book up, and limped into the bedroom brandishing it like a weapon.

'Morry, how could you –' I started to say as I opened the door. Then I stopped: for there he lay, fast asleep, with his lips parted in a broad smile and a paperback I hadn't seen before dangling limply from his hand. At that point, my heart melted with love for him. It's not his fault, I told myself, the man must be sick. It was at that moment I realized that reading is addictive. Then and there I resolved to get rid of every blasted book in the house. I crept forward and, carefully prizing open his fingers, took the paperback away. Holding both books at arm's length, I took them into the bathroom and made to throw them in the bin. As I did so, curiosity overcame me and I glanced at the covers. *Yet More Best Jewish Jokes* read one title. I flipped it open and glanced at a page.

Q. 'Why do Jewish husbands die young?'
A. 'Because they want to.'

With growing fear, I looked at the paperback. It was called *Oy, Mother! Oy, Mother!?* I opened it at the page where Morry had turned down the corner before he'd fallen asleep.

'Mervyn, I've pressed your socks for you, darling. So put them on, already.'

'I'm wearing some, Mom.'

'What's wrong? You don't like the way I pressed them? And Merv, you've tied your shoelace wrong. The bow'll come loose and you'll trip up. Here, let me re-tie it for you.'

'I can do it myself, Mom. I'm a big boy now. I'm forty-three years old.'

'To me, you'll always be my baby. And Merv, remember to call me when you get to this house where you're going to this party. I'll worry all night otherwise that you've been killed in a car wreck on the way.'

'No, Mom, I'm not gonna phone you.'

Frieda Rosenblum burst into tears. 'So, he doesn't care that I'll have a sleepless night not knowing whether my baby's alive or lying by the roadside, strangled by some crazy guy or shot dead in the street! These are dangerous times, Merv. It's only right that you should phone me . . .'

Of course it is, I thought, nodding in agreement. As I finished this page, and turned to the next one, my fears about Morry's reading habits slowly began to subside. At least he was not reading trash, but a serious book about a sensible woman that could, when I thought about it, only influence him for the better. After all, isn't he always criticizing me for being over-anxious about Robert and Sharon? And wasn't Frieda Rosenblum only saying almost word for word to her son what I often say to mine?

19

My reassurance lasted all of a minute. Then I remembered the broad smile on Morry's sleeping face, and the gales of laughter that had been issuing from the bedroom earlier that night. With growing apprehension, I read the reviews quoted on the cover.

'Not since *Portnoy* have the foibles of the Jewish Mother been more savagely exposed.' So the *New York Times* had said.

'Laugh? I nearly got a hernia!' *Los Angeles Magazine*.

'Frieda Rosenblum will go down in Literary History as one of the great comic Jewish characters of all time.' A comic character? I thought with shock. And this from our own *Jewish Chronicle*? How dare they! I said to myself, flushing with indignation. For if *Oy, Mother!* was supposed to be funny, it was an anti-Semitic, misogynist outrage. I stared at the author's picture with hatred. Who was this Daniel Z. Feigenbaum II? A young pip-squeak barely out of nappies. 'I only hope you have to bring up children of your own one day!' I said out loud. 'And I hope they play you up like my children have done me. Then you'll discover just what a "funny" business motherhood is!'

And what of the author's own mother? I wondered with an explosion of pity. How did the wife of Daniel Z. Feigenbaum I feel now that she was so exposed? These children, I thought, ought not to be allowed to get away with it. For it is a hard enough thing to be a mother nowadays without having all your caring efforts made into an international laughing stock. It is time we women showed our side of what goes on.

Though I have never been one to believe in vocations, what happened to me last Thursday night left me in no doubt but that I have something important to do before I die – to strike a blow in the defence of Jewish housewives.

What better way to do this than by telling, frankly and openly, the story of my own life? I can hardly wait to begin.

But how does one begin? Is there a skill to it? Does one just start at Page One and carry on until one gets to The End? Is an ordinary housewife like myself capable of doing it, or must one be a graduate like Sharon?

Capable or not, I made a start this week. First, I got Morry to teach me how to use the home computer that he keeps up here in Sharon's old bedroom (I am writing on it now). Second, I joined an evening class at our local Adult Education Institute, where I signed on for Creative Writing (Beginners) on Wednesday nights. I was delighted to see that the teacher is a Mrs Shirley Bloomstein. If anyone can help me to get even with the author of *Oy, Mother!*, I'm sure she can.

I rushed home from the Institute to tell Morry, who had just come in from work and was sitting in the lounge in his favourite armchair reading the evening paper. He glanced up at me for a split second, then disappeared back behind the paper. 'Hallo, darling,' he murmured. 'Did you have a good day?'

'I had a very good day,' I said pointedly. The paper rustled. 'Morry?' I said. 'Morry, did you hear me?'

'Mmm, Gloria?'

'Did you hear what I just said?'

'Of course. You said you had a very good day.'

'Well, don't you want to know what made it very good? Hmm, Morry? Morry, for God's sake put down that newspaper and talk to me a moment.'

He turned a page without looking up at me. 'I'm in the middle of a story,' he moaned.

'Morry!' I said more sharply. The paper lowered, and he stared up at me resentfully through his half-glasses.

'That's better,' I said. 'Sometimes I forget you have a face. All I ever see is columns and headlines.'

He sighed and folded the paper over. 'Is that all you wanted to say?' he said in a long-suffering voice.

'No, I . . . I just wanted to see you, that's all. After all, you are my husband. For all I know, there could be a perfect stranger sitting behind that paper. A rapist or a murderer.'

He lifted the paper again, mumbling, 'You'll turn me into a murderer one of these days.'

I was shocked. 'What kind of remark is that to make to your wife?'

'Only joking, Gloria.'

Was he? I looked at him – or rather at the sports page which was facing me. Why is it, I wondered, that my dear husband never listens to a word I say? Is he hard of hearing, or does he genuinely not realize that a wife needs to speak to her husband occasionally?

'Morry? Morry, darling!'

'Hmmm?'

'Must you read? I mean, you read a paper this morning.'

'This is the evening paper, Gloria,' said his muffled voice. 'A lot has happened in the world since then.'

Here was my opportunity to tell him. 'Yes, a lot has happened, Morry. I've joined an evening class at the local Institute.'

'Very nice, dear.'

I waited for a further reaction. 'Did you hear me, Morry?'

'Yes, dear,' he said without looking up. 'You said you'd joined an evening class at the local Institute.'

'Do you have to repeat everything I say? I mean, aren't you interested to know what in?'

He turned a page, somewhat impatiently. 'What in, Gloria?'

'In creative writing,' I confessed with some trepidation. 'I'm going to learn to become a writer. Morry, I want to write a book.'

Inch by inch, the paper lowered, revealing more and more of his incredulous face. 'You want to do what?'

'Don't you ever listen the first time? I said I want to write a book.'

There was a long silence, during which his jaw dropped a full two inches with astonishment. Then he burst out laughing. 'You've got to be joking!' he gasped.

1

Childhood,
the Happiest Days of My Life

Thursday, 11th September

Somewhere in Berwick Street in London's Soho, not far from the fruit-and-vegetable market, is the house where I, Gloria Gold, was born.

I simply cannot say that I was born in Soho in the first line of my autobiography. What will people think? That my mother was a prostitute? That I come from a long line of pimps? When the truth is that we were respectable Jewish working people with a small business making high-class evening gowns. But the readers won't know that when they read the first line, will they? They may even presume that I, Gloria Gold, am a prostitute. Far from it! I have only ever 'been with' one man, and that man is, of course, Morry. Naturally, I was a virgin when we got married. I say 'naturally' because in those days people just didn't behave the way they do now. Well, perhaps the men did, but the women didn't. If they did, you certainly didn't know about it. But in these permissive times, no sooner have they done it than they write about it in a magazine or a novel, or show it on television or the films.

To my mind, there's no need to go into these things in graphic detail. 'There's no need to pretend they don't exist, either,' says my dear daughter Sharon when she talks about such things as sex and, excuse me for mentioning it, menstruation, which she does often, sometimes during Friday night meals, which incidentally are the only times – infrequent though they may be – that I am on occasion blessed with having my two children sitting at my dining-room table, now that they have both left home.

'That's enough, Sharon!' I say.

'Why?' she says.

'I should have thought it was obvious,' I answer. 'It's not a fit discussion to have during a meal. It's embarrassing your father.'

'You're not embarrassed, are you, Dad?'

Biro in one hand and fork in the other, Morry will look up from the crossword clue he has been poring over and say, 'Sorry, Sharon? What was that?'

'See? Dad hasn't even been listening, have you, darling?' says Sharon victoriously.

'Well, then,' I say, 'you're embarrassing your brother.'

Torn between his love for his mother and sibling loyalty, Robert will crinkle up those deep-blue eyes of his and laugh loudly, saying, 'Don't bring me into this!'

'Robert doesn't mind, Mum,' Sharon continues, giggling with him. 'You're the only one who doesn't like talking about it.'

And thus pinned down, I usually turn the colour of the beetroot salad. 'Me?' I say. 'Don't be ridiculous. Why should I be embarrassed by talk about sex?'

Hold on a moment. What does all this have to do with my childhood? I'm digressing. I'd better start again.

I was born in London in 1930 . . .

That is no good either. I mean, how can I give away my age? Angel, my mother, who at seventy-nine admits only to sixty, will never forgive me. Neither will my 53-year-old sister Ruth. Also, my hairdresser Mario in the High Street will discover I've been telling him fibs all these years. I don't think I could take the humiliation when I next go in to have my tint done.

I was born in Edgware in 1931 . . .

I was born in the United Kingdom in 1932 . . .

I was born in England in 1933 . . .

I was born in 1940 . . .

I can already see that this is going to be a problem. Exactly what age should I make myself? If I make myself too young everyone will know I am lying. And if I make myself too old then I might as well tell the truth. Which, as it happens, is what my creative writing teacher at the Institute is expecting me to do.

I went to the first lesson last night, leaving Morry with a casserole in the oven. I walked into the classroom indicated on the Institute's noticeboard only to receive a terrible shock – Shirley Bloomstein, the teacher I'd been expecting, has had to give up teaching because of pressing commitments. Instead, the class is being taken by this Mr Foggart – a very tall, rather shambling man in his forties, with twinkly green eyes set in a somewhat rugged face and a wide mouth that seems to be constantly smiling.

My heart sank when I saw his Bohemian appearance –
those worn, corduroy trousers with the baggy knees, that
bristly chin, that shaggy pepper-and-salt hair – and then
again when he said his full name. *Christian* Foggart? Will
he understand a Jewish housewife wanting to get even
with Daniel Z. Feigenbaum II?

However disappointed I was, I decided that I ought to
be broadminded and stay for at least one class. So I took
my place with the other students, and listened to what he
had to say.

'The most important thing I'd like you to remember
when you're writing things to bring in to my class is to
try, above all, to be honest at all times,' he said as his eyes
swept over us (lingering, I noticed, on one or two of
the younger women students). 'Because in my opinion
honesty and integrity are most important – far more
important than style or talent. A writer – be he or she a
writer of fact or fiction – should be pledged to one thing
only, and that is to tell the truth.' And so saying, he
slipped off the desk he was perching on, and wrote *'Truth'*
in large, italic writing on the blackboard. At which we all
picked up our pencils and diligently copied this down.

I have just opened my notebook, and the word is there
before me in capital letters. TRUTH. Looking at it, I'm
beginning to feel guilty already. Does it mean I have to
mention Soho and give my age away? One can hardly
start an autobiography with two whopping lies. I suppose
the best thing would be not to bring up any controversial
subjects. I'll try again.

I was born.

There, that's better. But is it very interesting? Though it
is truthful, it could refer to anyone. Oh dear, I never

imagined writing a book would be so difficult. Mind you, it's not surprising, because at this time in the morning I can hardly see straight, let alone write. However, Mr Foggart says the only way to learn to be a proper writer is to get up an hour earlier every single morning and immediately sit down at the typewriter, before there is any time for 'resistance' to set in. So this morning I set the alarm for seven and crawled here into Sharon's room the moment I got out of bed.

Good God, just look at the time! Forty minutes have passed already! If it has taken me this long to write the first line, how long is it going to take to do a whole chapter?

What now, I wonder? Do I go on to describe every day of my life in detail? Or should I take a lead from the excerpts Mr Foggart read us out last night? For example, Marcel Proust, who ate a cake to summon up memories of his youth. Should I begin in the same vein? Somehow, a cream-cheese bagel doesn't sound as romantic as a madeleine. But a cream-cheese bagel is, in fact, the one taste that still takes me back to my childhood. Ruth and I would have them for tea every day when we were growing up, even though Nanny couldn't stand the sight of them. When Flora, our housekeeper, brought our tray up to the day nursery at four o'clock, Nanny would look at the bagels and turn up her nose, and demand that we be given cucumber sandwiches instead.

It makes me laugh now to think of this. But how could I ever put it in my autobiography? It would give a completely wrong impression of our house and the way we lived. Day nurseries, housekeepers and nannies – why, it sounds like we were gentry and lived in a stately home, when the truth was that we started off on three floors above the Soho factory, and then moved to a semi in

Edgware when I was seven years old. It just so happened that my mother was busy designing evening gowns for her and Daddy's business, Angel Dresses, which was why Ruth and I were brought up by what were then called 'staff'. And the day nursery was nothing more than one of the four upstairs bedrooms – the same room where Nanny slept at night.

Poor Nanny. I feel rather sorry for her. I think she felt that to live in the London suburbs and work for Jews was, somehow, beneath her. What did she think of us? I wonder. Did she like us at all? She used to say we drove her mad. And of course she did go mad in the end, stark raving bonkers, because of Mummy and her . . .

That's enough. I have just heard the lavatory flush. That must mean Morry is up. Yes, and it is eight o'clock already. Now I can stop writing and make breakfast and then begin the day's housework. Oh dear, I've been sitting here since seven and I've only three words to show for it. I wonder if that's a record?

Friday, 12th September

I can't stop yawning. Though I know that Mr Foggart said one has to get up early if one wants to be a writer, it does seem unnecessary punishment when one could theoretically find an alternative time to write during the day.

When, though? Today is Friday, one of the busiest days of the week, as any Jewish housewife knows. For on top of my ordinary work, I must do the shopping and cooking for tonight's dinner, and give the dining-room furniture a thorough going-over in preparation for the meal. 'Why so much effort when the table's going to be covered over by a cloth, Gloria?' Morry said when he caught me polishing its legs last night. 'What a waste of energy! After all, we're only going to be family.' 'It may be "only" family to you, Morry,' I said. 'But it's the most important thing in life to me.'

Mr Foggart is right, there's no way round it but to get up early. I'd better get a move-on.

I was born. My earliest memory is of being pushed in my pram around Regent's Park, with the smiling face of my dear Nanny beaming down at me.

This looks quite nice. However, now I look at it again, it certainly isn't true. My earliest memory is, in fact, of my grandmother giving me a chocolate. Come to think of it, I don't remember Nanny's face 'beaming down' when I was in my pram. I don't remember her smiling at all until Ruth was born. She certainly never smiled at me, no matter how hard I tried to please her.

Why have I lied about my earliest memory? What started yesterday with my age and birthplace seems to be becoming an unconscious habit. Just look at that one sentence. Good Lord, I've found another lie in it! Nanny never used to walk me to Regent's Park: she didn't think the air there was clean and insisted that nannies who took their charges to the Inner Circle were 'common'.

If Nanny was still alive she would think some of the people in my creative writing class were 'common' too. But common or not, they seem an interesting crowd to me. After having introduced himself to us as a professional novelist with a small reputation (he writes under a pseudonym which he mysteriously wouldn't tell us), Mr Foggart made us all stand up one by one and introduce ourselves to the rest of the class, and also to state what it was we were currently writing or wanting to write. To my horror he pointed at me first. Though I was trembling like a blancmange, I stood up and said clearly, 'My name is Mrs Gloria Gold, I'm proud to say that I'm a housewife, and I've come here to learn to write my autobiography.' At which no one laughed like Morry did when I told him. Instead they looked serious and nodded approvingly.

'You are brave, being the first one to stand up like that,' said a tiny lady called Mrs Balgrove when we sat at the same canteen table during the tea-break.

'Oh,' I lied. 'It was nothing.'

Mrs Balgrove told the class that she is seventy-two years old and that she took up writing short stories when her husband died five years ago. Apparently, she has already sold several stories to magazines, and named some obscure publications that Mr Foggart had never heard of. I must say, I was very impressed by her. It just goes to show that you should never judge a person by appearances. From her tight silver perm and thick crêpe stockings, you would never know she was a successful author. She looks more like a poor old dear for whom you would give up your seat on a bus.

Out of the whole class, she is the only one who has already been published – except an earnest-looking young man with a red wiry beard and an out-of-shape hand-knitted sweater called Gerrard Frobisher, who says he has written poetry all his life, and has recently 'gone professional' by having a 'haiku' published in a literary magazine. Sitting next to him was a rather upper-crust doctor, Dr Seal, who pronounces his name 'See-all', which I thought was rather amusing since he's so short-sighted he can hardly see anything. He described himself as an 'unpublished poet and novelist'. Then there are a very nice type of young lady called Melanie Thatcher who has been trying for years to get her romantic stories accepted by women's magazines and has so far met nothing but

rejection, a young secretary called Irene who wears skin-
tight jeans and wishes to write a play, and even a Brigadier
with an old-fashioned waxed moustache who is currently
working on the fifth volume of his so-far unpublished
memoirs.

All these people writing for years with no success, when
I am just beginning. It is rather dispiriting. How long
will I have to wait, I wonder, till I am published?

It is 7.47. I think I shall stop now, even though there
are, officially, thirteen minutes of my writing hour to go.
Looking back, I see I have now written about three lines
of my autobiography. How many more do I still have to
do?

Friday, 19th September

Eight whole days have passed since I started writing. And
what do I have to show for my efforts? A chapter heading,
two paragraphs and some useless notes I made after
talking to my mother yesterday.

'The trouble is that I've got such a short memory,' I
complained to Mr Foggart last Wednesday night. 'I can't
remember what happened to me yesterday let alone forty
years ago.'

'Forty years ago?' he said, frowning with disbelief.
'Surely you were no more than a babe in arms then, Mrs
Gold?'

'Oh, Mr Foggart! If only that were true!' I protested.

He gave me one of his wide smiles – the kind that
lights up his face and shows off his large, perfectly-
matched teeth. 'Surely an attractive young woman like
yourself . . .?'

'Oh, go on!' I laughed. 'Tell me, if one can't remember
things, what does one do?'

'One researches,' he said. I nodded knowingly. After all, I know all about research: it's sticking your nose into other people's business – what Sharon used to do in television before she became a big-shot producer who hasn't got time to see her parents. Mr Foggart then went on to say that I should talk to the people who knew me as a child and make notes which I can refer to when I'm writing. So after I'd done the housework yesterday, I phoned my mother Angel, and asked if I could go over and have a chat with her.

'What about?' she said suspiciously. 'You're not by any chance thinking of moving me into a home, are you? Because I've told you before and I'll tell you again, Gloria, I won't go, I won't. Just because I'm getting on doesn't mean I haven't got all my faculties. I'm as capable of looking after myself as you are. More so.'

'I know you are, Mummy,' I said. 'And you know I wouldn't dream of putting you in a home. Why, if a time ever comes when you can't manage alone, you'll move in with Morry and me.'

'No thank you!' she snorted. 'Five minutes in your house is enough to drive me mad. It's like being in a museum. I don't know how Morry stands it – everything stinking of bleach and draped in dust sheets!'

To tell the truth, by this time the vision of the cosy little chat I'd thought we were going to have had completely dissolved. 'I only try to keep the place clean,' I protested.

'There's clean and clean, Gloria. Homes are meant to be lived in, not preserved for posterity. Homes are like people – they are meant to grow old.'

Coming from Angel, who has had three face-lifts since her sixty-fifth birthday, this was some remark. It was then that I realized she must be joking. 'Oh, Mummy, you are funny!' I said, laughing with relief.

'Personally, I think you're pretty "funny",' she snapped back. 'I've never known anyone so obsessed by germs. You're running a house, not an intensive care unit.'

'Really! Just because I take pride in my housework!'

She sighed. 'Sometimes, Gloria, I don't believe you can be my daughter. I mean, how can anyone take pride in scrubbing a floor? Now, if you'd designed a beautiful dress, or painted a picture, or bought a lovely outfit cheaply in the sales, that would be something to take pride in. But scrubbing a floor? I'm proud to say I'd never scrubbed a floor in my life until I retired.'

'But then you always had a maid to do it for you, didn't you?' I pointed out.

'Of course I did! I had to, didn't I? Because, unlike you, I always worked.'

What does she think I do all day? Why does no one consider that housework is work any more? 'Are you a housewife, or do you work?' people ask me at parties – yes, and the worst culprits are career women like my mother and Sharon, and my old friend Claudia. I'd like to see them clean a house from top to bottom, not to mention do the laundry and buy and prepare a week of meals. Then they'd know what hard work is.

As far as I can see, there are two kinds of work – what you do for love, and what you get paid for. And if you do it for love, people expect you to be grateful for the opportunity. Well, I am grateful. Of course I am. With a wonderful family like mine, who wouldn't be grateful for the privilege of slaving away for them? But do they notice what I do for them, that's the question? Sometimes I wonder if Morry notices me at all. No wonder I nag him to put his books away – if I didn't, we'd never talk. I mean, he speaks to me sometimes – Yes darling, No darling – but it's not what I'd call a conversation.

I bet that Mr Foggart doesn't 'Yes-darling-no-darling' his wife. I bet he brings her flowers when he comes home at night, and introduces interesting topics and quotes from novels and biographies like he does in class. A man like that knows how to talk to women. He has that marvellous old-fashioned virtue we used to call 'charm', just like my brother-in-law Mark has.

Or should I say had until recently. When I popped into the Angel Dresses showroom on Monday to see Ruth, Mark was quite short with me. Have I done something to offend him? Perhaps I interrupted an important business discussion between him and that pretty young designer, Hattie, because he looked quite annoyed to see me, and fell unusually silent when I sat down with the two of them.

Why doesn't Morry talk to me properly? Sometimes I wonder if he wouldn't be happier with a housekeeper who just did the cooking and cleaning and otherwise left him alone. But then, of course, he'd have to pay a housekeeper, which I doubt he could afford, whereas I do it for free . . . Good God, I'm beginning to sound just like Sharon in her early feminist days! It must be my mood. I'm always a bit bad-tempered when I get up early in the morning.

It's 7.36. I feel really low and gloomy now. And I've a feeling this feeling is going to last all day. I thought that writing books was supposed to make you happier. What did Sharon say? That I needed something that would 'fulfil me as a person'. Frankly I felt a lot more fulfilled before I took up writing. Now I just feel angry and dissatisfied and cross with everyone including myself.

I'm bored with what I've written of Chapter One. Perhaps I'll scrap the bloody lot and start all over again.

But first let me get the rest of that telephone conversation with my mother off my chest. It's weighing on me, just like indigestion weighs on Morry every night.

'Surely you scrubbed a floor or two during the war, Mummy?' I insisted.

'I may have done, Gloria,' she said in a bored voice. 'To tell you the truth, it's not the sort of thing I remember. I did a lot of proper work during the war – fighting fires, designing uniforms, that sort of thing.'

'Housework is proper work too,' I said.

'Of a kind,' she muttered. 'There's no need to make it into a vocation. Haven't you got anything better to do than to nag your husband every time he puts his feet up on the coffee-table?'

I took a deep breath. Now was my opportunity to tell her. 'Yes, I have, actually. That's what I wanted to talk to you about.'

'Oh?'

'I've taken up writing.'

There was a short pause. 'What do you mean, you've taken it up?' she said.

'I mean I've joined a class. I'm learning to write.'

'Can't you write already? Didn't they teach you anything at school?'

Was she being deliberately provocative? 'What I'm talking about is creative writing,' I said, trying to keep the edge off my voice.

'Creative writing!' By the change in her tone I could see she was impressed. 'Now that does sound interesting. And what are you writing?'

'A book.'

'But I thought you hated them! Why, you wouldn't even come into the library with me the other day when I took my Harold Robbins back.'

'Of course not!' I said. 'That building is a fire-trap! I don't know how you can bear to go in there. And as for bringing their sticky, stained books into your own home . . . Really, Mummy, you could well afford to buy a new book if you needed one.'

'I don't know how I survived for so long without your advice, Gloria,' she said drily. 'And, for your information, one doesn't need books, one enjoys them.'

'I don't know how you can enjoy anything when you don't know where it's been! Library books are filthy.'

'Then perhaps you should get a job there, cleaning them up,' she said, stunning me into silence. I mean, when your own mother says such a thing to you! 'So, I gather you're not writing a *dirty* book,' she went on, chuckling at her pun. I said nothing. 'What kind of book are you writing?'

'My autobiography, actually.'

There was a long pause. Then, 'That ought to be interesting,' she said at last.

Was I imagining it, or was there a note of sarcasm in her voice? 'Yes, it will be,' I said. 'Actually, that's what I wanted to talk to you about.'

'About this book?'

'Sort of. About me.'

'You?' she said. 'What is there to talk about?'

I must admit, I felt quite affronted by this. All sorts of angry feelings welled up inside me. Then suddenly a funny thing happened – I was back in the day nursery in Edgware eating my high tea with Nanny and Ruth on one particular evening I haven't thought about in years. I must have been about ten years old when it happened. There I was in my woolly dressing gown, sitting at the table eating a boiled egg when Mummy and Daddy came sweeping in on their way out to the theatre, both dressed up to the nines. I had been going to tell them about the eight-out-of-ten I'd got for my composition at school, of which I'd been so very proud, but suddenly all the pride drained out of me. I looked at them, and then at my own face reflected in the back of my eggy spoon. How colourless and plain I looked compared to them! I knew then that however hard I tried I could never be as grand and exciting as they were without trying. I hung my head, and dear Daddy came over and kissed me on the cheek and asked me how school had been, and I never said a word about the composition.

What a funny thing memory is. Why should I suddenly remember that? I must have been quiet for some moments, because now my mother's voice was shouting down the telephone, 'Gloria? Are you still there? I said, what exactly about you?'

'Oh, this and that. You know, what kind of baby I was . . .'

'How am I expected to remember?' she interrupted. 'It was years ago. Besides, babies are all alike. What else?'

'Anything, really. Funny anecdotes about when I was little. Whether I slept well or had nightmares at night. Whether I splashed in the bath.'

'I wouldn't know,' she said. 'To tell you the truth, I never bathed you.'

I was shocked. 'What, never?'

'No, never. Nanny always did it.'

'Isn't that a bit strange?' I said. 'Didn't you ever want to?'

'No, not particularly. Should I have?'

'Well, isn't it natural for a woman to want to? I mean, bathing Sharon and Robert used to be such a delight.'

'I never had time for such pleasures,' Angel said. 'I had far too much work.'

There was that bloody word again: work.

Is it normal for a woman to feel so cross with her mother?

I must stop writing now. It's time to get Morry up and make him breakfast. Otherwise he'll be late for work.

Work.

I fear I've been neglecting the house lately. The carpet in this room needs an urgent Hoovering. I can't have done it since the day before yesterday. It's true what they say – a housewife's work is never finished.

Work, work, work.

Monday, 22nd September

It's 10.30, a lovely autumn morning outside, and I've been shut in this room since 9.15. And what have I accomplished during this time? I have

1. Paid my bills.

2. Phoned all the people to whom I owed telephone calls.

3. Sorted through all the computer disks one by one, deleting everything that wasn't important – and some things that were. All my 'morning writing' has disappeared down the wires. And so have Morry's household bills, and the record of our John Lewis account. Morry will be furious when he finds out.

In an hour and a half I must leave home to go down to Soho where I am having lunch with my old schoolfriend Claudia. Since Claudia is an editor in a publishing company I thought she might be able to give me a few professional tips about writing my autobiography. I do admire her. She's one of those wonderful Superwomen who manages to juggle a perfect marriage, a perfect job and perfect children, all three of whom are married. On top of this, she has a beautiful home in the middle of Hampstead which is constantly being redecorated in the latest style by Martin, her architect husband, her hair is immaculate and her designer clothes are always up-to-the-minute and spotlessly clean. She always looks wonderful, even when she wears those baggy, crumpled linen unstructured things straight out of the pages of *Vogue*. On her, they look just like they do on the models. Whereas on me I know they would look like they had just fallen out of a washing machine. But then, of course, Claudia has a fleet of dailies to clean her house, a fabulous bone structure and a perfect size eight figure, and anything looks good on her. Whereas I . . .

I have just been into my bedroom to have a look at myself in the mirror. I am not just 'cuddly' as the woman in Dickins & Jones dress department kindly said last week. I am getting fat, as Morry pointed out the other morning when I was walking across the bedroom in my bra and pants. On top of that, the subtle blonde tint Mario put on my hair the other day is uncomfortably close to bright apricot, and the set is too tight and, I'm afraid, somewhat old-fashioned. As for my clothes . . . I was wrong to think this printed M & S two-piece would do for another year. On reflection I don't think I should ever have bought it.

Oh God, I can't face seeing Claudia when I look like this! I know she'll look wonderful. Why do I suddenly feel so awful? I don't know why I'm going to meet her, I must be mad.

I was mad.

I was so afraid of not arriving on time at the trendy Soho restaurant which Claudia had chosen for our rendezvous that I got there half-an-hour early. She, on the other hand, arrived twenty minutes late, by which time I was already feeling I wanted to die. I was right about my hair. And about my appearance being frumpy. Not only did I look like the older generation, I felt like it too. In fact, I felt like a grandmother – which I could have been to half the whizz-kids lunching there on their expense accounts, were it not for the fact that neither Sharon nor Robert . . . No, I'm already too depressed to think about not being a grandmother. I can't go through all that again. Suffice it to say that I have already thrown that outfit in the dustbin, and am contemplating making an appointment with a new hairdresser in the West End. Mario isn't all he used to be, I'm afraid.

To say that Claudia's new look is somewhat understated would be an understatement. When she finally arrived (by which time I'd been through the contents of two bread-baskets and drunk half a bottle of wine) she looked like she'd just fallen out of bed. Granted she looked just like everyone else in the restaurant, but I was shocked when I saw her, really I was. She has let her hair go grey and has had it shorn almost to the scalp, with one long spiky lock left to flop down over her forehead. A pair of National Health wire-rimmed spectacles were perched on her nose. Surely she could afford to buy a decent pair of frames? She certainly earns enough, and so does Martin. As far as I could see, she wasn't wearing a scrap of make-up. A woman of her age – my age, for God's sake – needs at least a bit of rouge to brighten up those cheeks! As for that Japanese designer cotton coat – well, it looked just like Morry's old dressing-gown – the one I gave to the synagogue's charity bazaar.

So, I was wrong about her always looking wonderful. I suppose one could say she looked with-it, but . . . Surely a woman has a duty to society to make the best of herself, to do her face and show off her figure? Not that Claudia has a figure any more. When she shrugged off the coat, all that was left under the loose sack she wore beneath it was skin and bones and a neck that would have done justice to a boiling fowl. My first thought was, how tragic, she must have cancer. My second thought was, God, why did I eat all that bread before she came?

Everyone turned around to look at her as she walked into the room, and she must have said hallo and kissed about half a dozen people on the way over to the table. 'Darling!' she drawled in that deep gravelly voice the men always used to go so wild about when we were girls and went to dances together. 'I'm so sorry I'm late. Have you been waiting long? My editorial meeting went on for ever. I simply couldn't get away.'

'Oh, I'm sure it must have been interesting,' I said warmly.

'Christ no!' she sighed, throwing herself down on the chair. 'A deadly bore. You don't know how I envy you being a housewife! God, I'm dying for a drink.'

'Here, have a glass of this wine.'

'I never touch it,' she said with a shudder. (Frankly, I don't remember this from before. At her daughter's wedding she was practically under the table half the night. Mind you, that could have been because of the weight of those enormous diamond earrings she was wearing.) 'Alcohol ages the skin dreadfully, you know. Waiter! Perrier, please!'

She tilted her head back, so that she could see me through the spectacles, which were balanced right on the end of her nose, and I was treated to the first of many glimpses up her tiny nostrils. The loose skin between her eyebrows creased into a deep, displeased frown. Then, 'You look as wonderful as ever,' she said with a smile. 'How are you? And how is Morry?'

'Morry's fine. He's . . .'

'Dear Morry,' she muttered thoughtfully. Which I have to say left me feeling a bit surprised. I never thought she liked him. At least, not since that cocktail party when he'd asked her how old she was and then, when she'd tried to evade the question, he'd persisted till she'd lied.

The waiter came back, and greeted Claudia by name. She ordered first: fettucini in a fresh tomato and cream sauce followed by roast lamb with red-currants, cauliflower cheese and sauté potatoes. Casting caution and my diet to the wind, I decided to be sociable and order the same. But just as the waiter was leaving she called him back, saying she'd changed her mind, she wasn't really hungry, she'd like to cancel both courses and just have the crudités instead. What could I do? If I'd cancelled my order too it would have looked ridiculous. I remembered suddenly all those times when we were at school and she'd done the same thing in the sweet-shop round the corner, goading me on to have a double ice-cream cornet while she ended up having nothing at all. I never learn. Mind you, I have learned a lot at lunch today, viz:

1. If you want to make a good impression on someone, never order pasta in tomato sauce, especially if it contains long strands. My blouse is ruined.

2. When the waiter places a plate of fruit salad in front of you after your starter, never tell him that he's made a mistake and brought the pudding too early or you'll end up with egg on your face. There's bound to be some lamb underneath all that fruity embellishment. This is what is known in society as the Nouvelle Cuisine. And you can keep it, as far as I'm concerned. 'Six pounds ninety for *this*?' as I remarked to Claudia, spearing the postage stamp of meat on the end of my fork.

3. Never see Claudia again.

43

It's not that I don't like her. I mean, no one could say she isn't marvellous. It's just that . . . just that . . . She's so intelligent. She's so capable. And she has such style – *she*'d never get tomato sauce on her blouse. Just looking at her makes you think, why even try to make yourself look nice? Why even pretend that you could be anything but the boring, suburban housewife you are? You might as well give up right now. Because she's done it all already *and* done what I've done as well – brought up children, made a lovely home, been a good wife, even raised money for charities. On top of this, she's such a nice person. I must be wicked to hate her so much.

By the time we'd – or rather I'd – eaten (you could hardly call the way she toyed with those little carrot sticks eating) I was feeling thoroughly demoralized. I'd asked her about her family, and she'd shown me photographs of her five grandchildren. She'd asked me about my family, and I'd shown her nothing. What could I show her – a photo of Sharon's cat? I did my best to make things sound all right – skirted all the worst bits and told her about the new flat Robert is buying, and Sharon's job in television. 'I always did like Robert,' she said, looking at her Rolex watch. 'Such a handsome, gentle boy. And Sharon, too. You must be terribly proud of her. She's done so well for herself, and she's always such fun.' Fun? My Sharon? Were we talking about the same girl? 'Do you know, in a strange way, I almost wish she was my daughter,' Claudia added wistfully. You can have her, I thought, and I hope she brings a little more pleasure to your life than she's done to mine.

When we'd exhausted the family, she asked me what I had been up to. I had not yet dared to mention my writing ambitions to her, but here at last was my chance. My heart was beating pit-a-pat with a strange excitement, and to calm myself, I took another sip of wine. As I put my glass down, I glanced at the bottle, and realized to my horror that it was completely empty. Since Claudia was drinking Perrier, that could only mean one thing. Suddenly the room started spinning, and my face flushed hot with fear. I blotted my forehead and, with difficulty, focused my eyes on Claudia. 'I've joined a creative writing class,' I blurted out with none of the subtlety I'd planned. 'I'm writing a book.'

All the warmth and charm she's famed for in our social circle suddenly drained from Claudia's face. 'Well, well, how interesting, Gloria,' she said after a short pause.

'Yes it is, it is . . . You see, I've always felt I had something to say, you know, deep down inside.'

'Most people do feel that,' she said rather frostily, glancing at her Rolex again. 'However, only a very few of them actually do have anything worth saying.'

'I thought you might . . . I mean . . .' I hesitated.

Her eyes widened in horror. 'Good God, darling, you're not going to ask me if I'll publish it, are you?'

'Of course not! I mean I wouldn't dream of presuming . . .'

A sigh of relief escaped from her pursed lips. 'Thank God, Gloria. You had me worried there. Believe me, mixing business and pleasure is always a mistake. Christ knows the ghastly manuscripts I've had thrust upon me in the name of friendship. Not that your manuscript is ghastly. I'm sure it's absolutely marvellous.' Thoroughly flustered, I picked up my empty wine-glass and tried to drink from it. 'Here, have some Perrier,' she said, pouring me a glass. 'It'll do you the world of good.'

I gulped it down and, to my embarrassment, burped loudly. 'Of course I wasn't going to ask you to publish it

– yet,' I added, just in case I ever want to change my mind. 'I just wanted to ask your advice, that's all. After all, you are a professional . . .' The warmth returned to her face, '. . . and I am just a beginner, and I've never done anything like this before.'

'Darling, you can have advice any time, any time, as much as you want. Only . . .' She glanced at her watch for a third time. 'Oh Lord, is that the time? I've a meeting in fifteen minutes.' But seeing my distressed expression, she threw her hands up in the air with that girlish laugh I've always loved her for. 'Oh, bugger the meeting!' she exclaimed recklessly. 'Tell me about it now. How far have you got with it?'

'Well, I'm sort of starting,' I said cautiously.

'Darling, that's marvellous. Remember that even Tolstoy had to start *War and Peace* once upon a time. And what kind of book do you plan to write? Poetry? Fiction? Or perhaps a biography?'

I blushed. 'Actually I was thinking more in terms of an autobiography,' I mumbled.

'What?'

'Auobiography. You know, the story of my life.'

'Your life,' she repeated. There seemed something ominous in her tone of voice. 'That's very interesting. However, if you're writing with a view to publication – which you are, I suppose, aren't you?' I nodded, and her face fell again. 'Well, darling, in that case don't you think you'd be better off to stick to fiction?'

'But why?'

For the first time since I've known her – which is almost half a century – she looked genuinely nonplussed. 'Well, because fiction is a little easier than autobiography,' she said at last, with an unconvincing smile.

I felt my heart sink. After all, I've been getting quite

excited about writing my life story. 'Don't you think I'm up to it, then?' I asked, bracing myself for her answer.

She picked up the wine bottle, poured the last dregs into her glass and drank them down without hesitation. 'Of course I do, Gloria. Don't get me wrong. I know you'd write a marvellous autobiography. It's only that, professionally speaking . . .' She bit her lip.

'Yes?'

'Well, professionally speaking, I . . . I tend to think that autobiographies are best left to those who've done something with their lives – preferably something rather important.' Though I tried to stop them, tears of humiliation welled up in my eyes. 'You know,' Claudia went on, looking so upset now that I would have felt quite sorry for her had I not been so busy feeling sorry for myself. 'Like climbing Everest or building a financial empire or winning the Nobel Prize or . . .' Silence fell. With a deep sigh she signalled desperately to the waiter to bring us the bill, which she insisted on paying. 'Darling, much as I'd love to carry on talking I just have to go back to work now,' she said, clasping my hand in her bony, ring-studded fingers. I nodded without looking up. 'But call me up soon – very soon, as long as it's after next week – and we'll discuss it again. And don't let me put you off. I'm sure whatever you eventually decide to write will be fascinating, really. Really, Gloria. Oh God. Here, have my handkerchief. No, that's all right, I don't want it back, save it for next time we meet. And then perhaps you'll give me your manuscript, and I'll have a look at it. I'd love to, really. And don't take it so personally, darling,' she finished off, her sympathy tinged with a flash of annoyance. 'I mean you did ask for my professional advice, didn't you?'

I must have been mad.

Thursday, 2nd October

It has been ten days since I had lunch with Claudia – ten days in which I haven't written a word. Mr Foggart was most disappointed with me last night, when I admitted that yet again I'd brought nothing to read out in front of the writing class. I think he's realized that my commitment to Literature doesn't stretch very far. What little enthusiasm I once had for writing an autobiography had all disappeared by the time I sobered up last Monday afternoon. And no wonder: I mean, what is the point of struggling to write a book when no one's going to want to publish it when it's finished? Because, as Claudia implied, nothing I've done in my fifty-six years is important enough to be of interest to anyone else.

How times have changed! Why, when I was a child, being a housewife was considered important in itself. People admired such a woman, vacated their seats for her on the bus, and men even gave her money from their wagepackets so she could run the home. Nowadays the 'clever' thing is to be independent: to have a job instead of a baby; to stand strap-hanging on the tube with half a dozen carrier-bags of shopping weighing down your arm so that some man can have what ought by common decency to be your seat; to work like a slave at a 'career' so you can afford to pay half the household bills yourself instead of having them paid by your husband. What's so clever about all that, I'd like to know? I mean, who in their right minds would pay a bill if they didn't have to?

So, my experience is unimportant, my lifestyle is boring, and being a housewife and mother has been a complete waste of time. Never mind that without me to fill their tummies, wash their clothes, make their beds, sweep their floors, nag them into behaving properly and generally set them an example of a decent way of life, *none* of my family – neither Morry nor Robert, nor for that matter Sharon, for all she talks about standing on her own feet – would ever have done what they've done, or become what they've become.

On second thoughts, perhaps that wouldn't have been such a bad thing. After all, aren't I always saying I wished they were different – that Morry talked more, that Sharon had more sense, that Robert was . . . that Robert wasn't . . . that he was less difficult to please when it came to girlfriends? Oh God, I don't think I've ever felt so un-happy. Perhaps it's all my fault that their lives are turning out such a mess.

And perhaps I'd have been happier too if I'd been a mountaineer, or an explorer, or even a publisher like Claudia. And perhaps if I'd been less selfless in my de-votion to my family, they'd have been more appreciative of what I've done for them over the years.

Listen to me, what am I saying? I am happy, of course I am. Who wouldn't be, with a wonderful husband like Morry and two wonderful children like Robert and Sharon, not to mention my Honda Civic and my lovely semi-detached Hendon house? I ask you, what more could a woman want in life? More money? Health is better than wealth, that's what my darling father Harry used to say. A size eight figure like Claudia's? Perhaps. Maybe. Married children? I admit that would be a bless-ing. A husband who talks to me? Yes, that would be nice. In fact, when I come to think of it, I'd like a lot of things to be different.

In my heart of hearts, I always knew that Literature was subversive. Just see how dissatisfied I've already become!

Tuesday, 7th October

I am quickly coming to the conclusion that a writer needs an office to write in, for there are too many distractions from 'being creative' at home. First, there's the housework. Second, people seem to think that because you're at home you're just sitting there waiting for them to ask you to do things for them. Take yesterday, for example. I had planned to rush through my household tasks as quickly as I could so that I could spend the entire afternoon making a fresh start on Chapter One. And what happened? First my mother phoned, and asked me to pick her up and drop her at the hairdresser's. Then when I came back from dropping her, my sister Ruth rang up twice from Angel Dresses, the first time to ask me to pop out to the shops and buy her a chicken since she had no time to get out of the showroom herself, the second time (when I'd come back from the butcher's) to ask me to roast it.

'Plenty of herbs, no salt and no extra chicken fat,' she said. 'Mark's on a diet.'

'What sort of diet is this with no salt and no fat?' I said. 'Would you like me to make sure the chicken has no taste too?'

'You may laugh, Gloria,' she said in a harassed voice. 'But Mark's had high blood-pressure lately, and the doctor told him to cut down on salt and cholesterol. Which you ought to, too. Morry could do with a healthier diet.'

'A little chicken fat and seasoning never did anyone any harm,' I said. 'Remember, Ruth, we Jews have survived for thousands of years by eating traditional food. You're beginning to sound like my Sharon with these fads of yours. One week it's brown rice with everything, the next it's flavourless chicken!'

'It won't be flavourless if you sprinkle some herbs on it.'

'Herbs!' I sneered. 'I've never cooked with herbs in my life.' And I haven't, I'm proud to say. Good, plain cooking is my forte: chopped liver, cream of mushroom soup, roast chicken, meatballs and noodles, beef stew, veal goulash – all prepared with plenty of butter and pure chicken fat in the wholesome, traditional way.

'Well, perhaps you should start,' she said. 'Herbs are essential. All those Frenchwomen can't be wrong.'

'Frenchwomen?' I shuddered. 'What do they know?' Ever since she and Mark started taking their holidays in the South of France, Ruth's been going on and on about French cooking and how wonderful it is. Well, I've been to France too, and one trip to a restaurant lavatory is enough to put you off their 'cuisine' for life.

Ruth sighed down the telephone line into my ear. 'You know I don't like to ask you, Gloria,' she said rather crossly. 'After all, I know how busy you are. I wouldn't have asked if I wasn't so desperately busy myself. A dress collection doesn't design itself, you know.'

Here it comes again, I thought: this business of work. Not that my sister doesn't work hard. She never stops. Without her, Angel Dresses would have fallen apart long ago, even though when my mother retired a few years ago she insisted on handing over her position of managing director to Mark. Because although Mark is a dear, handsome man, I'm afraid that he has a tendency to fecklessness and often wanders out of the showroom during the working day, leaving Ruth not only to design all the dresses and organize the staff, but also to serve the retail buyers who come in as well. 'I thought you'd taken on an extra designer to help with the collection this year,' I said.

'Hattie? She's hopeless,' Ruth said.

'Really?' I said. 'Well, in that case why don't you get rid of her?'

There was a moment of silence. Then, 'I suppose she's all right. Mark thinks she's good,' she said in an off-hand manner. Suddenly she seemed to lose her temper. 'Look, forget roasting the bloody chicken if it's too much trouble,' she snapped. 'I stupidly thought that since you were sitting at home in the house with nothing to do all day it would be easy for you to stick it in the oven. Obviously I was wrong. So just forget it. Mark and I will go out for dinner instead.'

'And waste money on God-knows-what rubbish in a restaurant?' I said, feeling awfully guilty by then. 'I'll do it, Ruth, I'll do it, darling. I never said I wouldn't. I mean, what else are sisters for? I just don't have any herbs.'

Suddenly her whole tone of voice changed and she seemed on the point of tears. 'Darling, parsley will do,' she choked. 'You've got some of that, surely? Well, loosen the skin and stuff a few sprigs between the breast and the thigh. And if you've got time, you could marinate the whole bird in a little lemon juice and crushed garlic before you cook it. And rub a pinch of mustard into the skin. Would that be all right? Oh, you're an angel, Gloria! Whatever would I do without my family? I really don't know.'

And whatever would I do? I thought when I hung up. I'd probably have some time to myself. As it was, a few minutes later my mother phoned again, saying it was raining and she couldn't get a taxi back from the hair-dresser's, so could I possibly collect her? And when I eventually got home after dropping her home, I had to spend the rest of the afternoon in the kitchen basting Ruth's fatless fowl with water to make sure it didn't burn.

'I hope it's okay,' I said to her as I handed it over in its baking tray.

She lifted the foil and sniffed underneath. 'Gloria, it smells wonderful,' she said, and kissed me on the cheek. 'You're a good cook and a marvellous sister. I hope it wasn't any trouble.'

'It was a pleasure,' I assured her. 'Any time you want something doing, give me a call.'

Was Ruth all right? I wondered as she walked down the garden path towards her car, her shoulders hunched beneath her huge shoulderpads? Was I mistaken, or had she been crying? If not, why the sun-glasses when it was dark out? And why did Mark not come in with her to collect the chicken, but only wave from the car window? When I told Morry about this, he told me not to be ridiculous. 'They were probably both tired, Gloria. Forget it. Stop panicking.'

'I'm not panicking, I'm just worried.'

'So what's new?' Morry said, selecting a book from the pile beside his armchair. 'You're always worried. Ruth's fine, believe me. Perhaps she and Mark have had a tiff. That's not so terrible, is it? Find something else to worry about.'

Actually, I am worried about something else: my writing class tomorrow night. What will Mr Foggart say when he finds out I still haven't got any further with my autobiography? I'm so afraid to tell him I almost feel like not going.

I wonder what happened to my 'vocation'. I'll never get even with Daniel Z. Feigenbaum II at this rate.

Thursday, 9th October

There was so much going on in class last night that I thought for a time Mr Foggart had forgotten I'd promised to bring in my first chapter: Melanie Thatcher read out the beginning of a short story she is currently writing about a blind composer and his widowed secretary who fall in love while on a Greek Islands cruise; then Dr Seal recited a poem he'd written about his old dog, Cracker. After the tea-break everyone discussed what we'd heard. For some strange reason, Mr Foggart was being particularly critical of what he called Melanie's 'overliberalness with the adverbs', and also of Dr Seal's poem, which he called 'sugary'. I couldn't help feeling a little sorry for the poor doctor. After all, he is a widower and Cracker, who was run over last week, had been his only companion for the last eleven years. If Christian is in such a bad mood, I thought, it's a good thing he's forgotten to ask me to read my work.

But he hadn't forgotten. At the end of the evening, just when everyone was going home, he cornered me by the blackboard.

'Mrs Gold, why haven't you brought in any work yet?' he said, fixing me with one of the hard smiles he always wears when he's being particularly critical. 'Is it that you feel too self-conscious to read it out, or are you still having difficulty in beginning it?'

The door swung shut behind the last departing student, and we were alone together. I braced myself for an attack as he towered over me. 'Of course I've begun it,' I lied quickly. 'Actually, I've written quite a bit this week. In fact, I was meaning to bring it with me tonight, but I did the most stupid thing – I left it behind at home.'

He raised his eyebrows. 'Mrs Gold!' he drawled slowly in a deprecating way.

I blushed deeply. 'Mr Foggart,' I blustered. 'You don't seem to believe me!'

'Saying one has left one's writing at home is the oldest trick in the book,' he said. At this, my mouth dropped open with shame and I truly did not know what to say. He must have sensed my dismay, because he suddenly cracked his hard smile, slouched against the wall, and laughed confidentially. 'I only know this because I've made that same excuse many times in the past myself!'

'Have you really?' I said, astonished out of my embarrassment.

He shrugged his very broad shoulders, and stuffed his hands into the baggy pockets of his trousers. 'Do you think each and every one of us doesn't suffer from writer's cramp at some time or other?'

I took a deep breath and decided to come clean with him. 'Cramp?' I said. 'To me it's more like permanent paralysis.' He laughed heartily. 'I'm glad you think it's amusing,' I said. 'It feels terrible to me. In fact, I don't think I can carry on with creative writing much longer.'

'Oh no!' he moaned. 'You're not planning to drop out of my class? But you can't, Mrs Gold! I should be heartbroken. I should miss your contributions.'

Now it was my turn to look sceptical. 'But I never say anything,' I said. Now he looked embarrassed. 'You know, there's a word in the Yiddish language for false flattery,' I went on. 'It's called *shmooze*.'

A faint blush crept into his cheeks and he raised his eyebrows and said, 'I didn't realize you were Jewish.'

'With my face?' I retorted. 'Funny, I thought writers were meant to notice these things.' He looked a bit upset when I said this, so I added quickly, 'I'm sure a real

55

novelist like you has more important things to think about than whether or not his students are Jewish. But when you're Jewish, you see, that's the first thing you notice about a stranger.'

'Really?' he said, sitting down on one of the desks. 'I didn't know that. How do you tell?'

'Oh . . .' A thousand things crowded into my mind, but I hesitated to say any of them. The expression on a person's face, the shape of their nose, their choice in make-up and jewellery, the cut of their clothes, the way they speak to or look at you with a certain guarded curiosity in their eyes as they wonder if, or realize that, you too are Jewish like them – these are not the kinds of things you can explain to someone who isn't. 'It's difficult to describe,' I said at last. 'You just know. Let's say it's a kind of mental Masonic handshake.'

'My, what a hidden talent you have, Mrs Gold!' he exclaimed. 'An excellent analogy. You ought to write it down and use it in your book. If you don't, I will. You'll be plagiarized before you're published!'

'Mr Foggart,' I said. 'I'm sure a professional writer like yourself has no need to steal from a beginner like me.'

'Writers are notorious thieves, Mrs Gold,' he teased. 'You have to be careful what you say in front of them!'

'Oh, Mr Foggart, you are funny!'

'Look, can't we dispense with this Mr Foggart–Mrs Gold business?' he said. 'You do realize you're the only one in the class who doesn't call me by my "Christian" name?'

'That must be because I'm Jewish!'

When we'd both stopped laughing at each other's jokes, he suddenly became serious again. 'Well, Gloria, why haven't you been able to make a start on your writing yet? Is the paralysis complete?'

'Almost.'

'And are you doing your morning writing exercises as I asked you to? Are you getting up an hour early?'

'Every day. Well, almost every day. I started off that way, but . . .' I shook my head. 'If I do or I don't, it doesn't seem to make much difference. You see, I get side-tracked the moment I start.'

Suddenly his smile collapsed. 'Mmm. I know that feeling,' he groaned.

'Do you?' I asked in surprise.

'Only too well. There are always distractions when you're working at home, especially when your wife –' He stopped suddenly, cleared his throat and looked up to me, hoisting his fallen features into a watery smile. 'What happens when you get sidetracked, Gloria? Do you stop writing or what?'

'Sometimes,' I said. 'Other times I just end up writing down whatever comes into my head.'

His face lit up. 'Why, but that's terrific!' he said. 'That's just what we're after!'

'What do you mean?' I said apprehensively.

'That's what it's all about – writing straight from one's unconscious mind. Believe me, it's the way the most valuable thoughts and ideas emerge. That's pure creation – what we call in the trade "inspiration".'

'Nonsense,' I said. 'It's just drivel. You should see it.'

'I'd like to, very much,' he said. 'Why don't you bring it in next week?'

I looked horrified. 'I couldn't!'

'Why not?'

I thought of what I've written about Sharon and Robert and nagging Morry. The idea of reading that in public was horrendous. 'It's far too personal,' I protested.

His mouth twitched. 'An autobiography can hardly be impersonal, Gloria.'

'Yes, but –'

'The whole joy of literature is that it speaks the truth.'

'No one else would be interested in my home truths,' I said. 'Anyway, they're private.'

'The truth belongs to no one,' Christian said. 'It speaks to all people. It is universal.'

'I see,' I said, although by this time he had lost me completely.

'So pluck up your courage, and bring some of that "unconscious writing" in next week,' he coaxed.

I nodded. When he looked at me that way, how could I refuse him? Just then the classroom door swung open, and the face of that young blonde, Irene, appeared. 'Oh, there you are, Christian! Still here? We've been waiting for you outside the front door. Aren't you coming to the King's Head tonight?'

'I'll see you there, Irene,' Christian said. 'I'm just giving a bit of advice to Gloria.'

'Well, don't keep him too long, Mrs Gold,' she said, withdrawing.

'You know,' I said as we left the room, 'I'm sure I could write the whole book if I could only get past the beginning. But I just don't know how to start my chapters.'

'Starting is a tricky business, isn't it?' he said as we walked slowly down the corridor together. 'I mean, one wants to engage the reader as quickly as possible, while setting the whole tone of the piece. You know, sometimes it helps to start on, say, the second chapter, and leave writing the very beginning until you've reached the end. And I tell you what, it's worth having a look at how other writers handle their first pages. Go back to the classics.

Take a look at how your favourite authors manage to begin their chapters. Dickens, Austen. What are your favourite books, by the way?'

'I don't have any,' I said derisively.

He stopped and looked at me strangely. 'What do you mean?'

'I mean I don't . . .' Suddenly a funny thing happened to me: for the first time in my life I felt ashamed to say that I don't like books. What's the matter with me? I wondered. It is something I've always been so proud of. But somehow I knew that Christian wouldn't understand. 'I mean, I don't have any favourites,' I said quickly. 'I'm not a discriminating reader.'

'Well, I'd never have known that, Gloria,' he said, throwing his battered leather satchel over his shoulder and gazing straight into my eyes. 'You strike me as a woman of strong tastes.'

2

On the Brink of Womanhood

Friday, 10th October

Last night I dreamed I was in Edgware again. It seemed
to me I stood outside the door of our house, waiting
to go inside, and for a while I could not get in because
it was barred to me. I called in my dream to Nanny,
and had no answer, and peering closer through the
letterbox I saw that the hall was empty and the house
uninhabited . . .

I was the best of teenagers, I was the worst of
teenagers . . .

It is a truth universally acknowledged (by all but my
daughter) that a single girl not in possession of a good
fortune must be in want of a husband.

It was a bright cold day in April and the clocks were
striking one . . . two . . . three . . . four . . . five . . .

Oh, what bloody difference does it make? So *Nineteen
Eighty-Four* is what they call a 'Classic of Literature' is it?
And this is supposed to be a good beginning? I've never
heard a clock strike thirteen in my life! If you ask me, that

60

entire, grubby, unpleasant trip to the library yesterday afternoon was a complete waste of time!

Saturday, 11th October

Why am I sitting here pretending I want to be a writer when my only real ambition is to be a grandmother?

Hannah Cohen, a very nice lady who is often at Mario's at the same time I am, showed me a photograph of her eight grandchildren when we were sitting under the driers yesterday. Eight grandchildren! And Hannah's eldest daughter, Karen, is only Sharon's age!

'She started young. I tried to persuade her to finish college before she got married, but she wouldn't listen,' Hannah confided. '"Mum," she said, "I know how much joy getting married and having children brought you and Dad, and I can't wait to do the same myself."'

'Count your blessings,' I told Hannah. 'Your daughter has done the right thing. Not that I don't believe in education but . . . What did she need to go to college for? You don't have to be a graduate to know how to operate a washing machine.'

The photograph was taken at Hannah's eldest grandson's barmitzvah, and to tell the truth it brought tears to my eyes. I took one look at the boys in their skullcaps and the girls in their dainty party dresses, all gathered around Hannah and her husband, and I thought, even if Sharon got pregnant today, by the time her first child reached barmitzvah age it's unlikely Morry and I would both be alive to hear him read his portion of the Torah. After all, we're not getting any younger. And neither is Sharon. Her womb must be shrivelling up inside that flat belly of hers. She'll never have children if she doesn't start soon. And unless she starts soon, I won't be around to enjoy them. It's not fair, it really isn't. Why do other women get pleasure from their children, when all I get from mine is aggravation? Oh, I'm so jealous of Hannah I could die!

However, one very good thing came out of our chat: it appears that she's got a nice niece in Manchester who's coming down to stay with her in a fortnight's time.

'A lovely girl,' she said. 'Marilyn. A legal secretary.'

'Very nice,' I said. 'How old is she?'

'Twenty. Twenty-something. What does a year here or there matter? A lovely fresh young girl, believe me. Lives at home with her mother.'

'Really?' I said. 'That's unusual in this day and age.'

Hannah nodded. 'It's a grave mistake to let them leave home till that wedding band is welded on to their finger.'

'Don't I know it?' I sighed. 'Why, if I had my time all over again . . .'

'But what can you do?' Hannah said. 'They've got minds of their own, unfortunately.'

'Don't I know it?' I sighed again.

'Anyway, Marilyn's saving up for a deposit so she can buy a little flat when she gets married.'

'Ah, a sensible girl. Thinks of the future.'

'Not that she needs to save, of course. She's an only child, and my brother-in-law is a successful jeweller.'

'Very nice,' I said, suddenly thinking of my Robert. If only he'd settle down with a girl like that! 'Is she pretty?' I asked.

Hannah clucked. 'She's a doll, a real doll. Auburn hair, brown eyes. Lovely teeth. Dainty features. A beautiful girl, believe me. All the boys are after her.'

'I'm sure they are,' I said wistfully.

There was a short pause. 'I was wondering, Gloria . . .' Hannah said.

'Yes?'

'You see, Marilyn doesn't know anyone here in London – I mean, she knows us of course, but she doesn't know anyone of her own age. I'd like to introduce her – you know, so she could go out a bit with other youngsters. Anyway, I wonder whether you might know a few people I could introduce her to, seeing as you've got single children yourself. I'm not matchmaking, you understand – the girl's got offers enough in Manchester. I just wanted to find someone she could go out with while she's down here, to have a little fun with. And if anything more were to develop, well and good. I'm sure my sister would be delighted.'

My heart leapt. 'I'm sure my Robert would like to meet her,' I said, and there and then made an arrangement for Marilyn to come over one Friday night for supper.

Have I done the right thing? I doubt it, knowing Robert. I've introduced him to girls before, and somehow it has never worked. Still, I suppose I've nothing to lose by trying. Perhaps he'd be different if he met the right person. I can't understand why he doesn't have women falling over him. At least, I don't think he does. If he does he never mentions them. He's never brought one home. Might that be because he's ashamed of them? Because he knows I won't approve? Because they're what Nanny would have called 'common', or not Jewish? Dear God, believe me, I don't mind if he's seeing *shikses* – it'd be a relief just to know he's seeing girls.

Monday, 13th October

I've been walking on air ever since I invited this Marilyn to dinner, because I am convinced that this time my matchmaking plans will work. Every time I close my eyes

I can see Robert's wedding: the synagogue full of the family; the bridesmaids carrying posies of pink roses; Marilyn floating down the aisle in a long white organza dress on her father's arm. I wonder if she'll want Sharon to be a bridesmaid? I'm afraid she'd be more of an old maid than a bridesmaid. Still, you never know: just maybe Marilyn has a distant relative who's handsome and single and who likes difficult women, and he'll notice Sharon in the synagogue and fall in love with her instantly, and propose during the reception. Oh, wouldn't that be wonderful? To get rid of both my children in one go!

Where would we hold Sharon's wedding reception? And what would I wear? The same outfit I'd worn for Robert's? What food would we get the caterers to serve? Knowing Sharon, she'll want something different – a vegetarian banquet, probably, with lentil sandwiches and brown rice croquettes. What will my friends say when they see such peculiar food on the buffet table?

Of course it'll be up to Hannah's sister and brother-in-law where Robert and Marilyn's reception takes place. It is the duty of the bride's parents to arrange these things, after all. I wonder if I'll like them. I wonder if they'll like me. I wonder if Marilyn's cousin who's going to fall for Sharon comes from a nice family. I wonder if he's rich, and what he does for a living. A dentist, or an accountant, or even – yes! – a doctor. If he's a doctor, he must have a practice in Manchester, which means that Sharon will have to give up that job when she moves up North to live with him. And if she gives up that job, she's bound to have a baby. What else will she do when she's a married woman? Oh, how marvellous – I'm going to be a grandmother at last. Hurrah, hurrah, hurrah!

I'm getting carried away. After all, Marilyn may not have a cousin, and Robert hasn't even met her yet. For all I know they may not even like one another when they do meet. Naturally, if she's got any sense, Marilyn will like Robert. But the main thing is, will he like her? Does he ever like women? If not, what instead? The consequences of that don't bear thinking about. Oh dear, my elation of the past few days has suddenly gone. I'm beginning to feel depressed again.

3

Love, Marriage and the Home: a Woman's Rightful Place

Wednesday, 15th October

Since I was getting nowhere with Chapter Two I've decided to make yet another fresh start today, and begin Chapter Three. Which is really quite far along the road to finishing my autobiography. Chapter Three! I never thought I'd get this far so quickly. I'm really quite delighted with my progress. Suddenly there is light at the end of the tunnel, and I'm beginning to imagine I might one day finish the thing.

I suppose that once I'm published and my face is on a book jacket it won't be long before I'm recognized in public places. I can just imagine it now, as I wheel my trolley round Waitrose: instead of walking right past me and butting me in the ribs with their wire baskets as they do now, my fellow shoppers will stop at a respectful distance, then they'll come up to me, smiling shyly and say, 'Excuse me for asking, but aren't you the woman who wrote that marvellous book about being a wife and mother?' And when I'm in the High Street I'll be ushered to the front of the fishmonger's queue, and if anyone complains, Mr Klein behind the counter will wipe his gutting-knife menacingly on his apron and murmur, 'Don't you know who that is? It's Gloria Gold! She's a big-shot writer now. She's got better things to do with her time than stand gossiping here with you.'

Does this sound a little conceited? I must be careful not to let success go to my head. After all, I'll always be proud to be an ordinary housewife, no matter how famous I become. Also, when I come to think about it, the book hasn't actually been accepted by a publisher. Another thing, I haven't written it yet. And unless I get down to it soon, this writing hour will pass in messing around like all the others have, and Chapter Three will end up in the dustbin – the same place as Chapters One and Two.

So let me make a start while I'm feeling enthusiastic.

Careers may come and careers may go, but when it comes down to it, nothing is as lasting and as fulfilling for a woman as a good, solid, happy marriage founded on mutual respect, honesty and love.

Christian will be pleased with this sentence, won't he? It is nothing if not true. Because what kind of life can a woman lead if she isn't married? For example, what would I do with myself all day, if there was not a man in my life for whom to cook and clean? What, for another example, does that daughter of mine do all day besides produce a half-hour television programme every now and then? 'What are you doing tonight, darling?' I ask when I ring her at work every afternoon. 'I'm going out with friends,' she says. What friends? What are their names? Have I ever met one? Of course not. Why should I when, as she keeps telling me, she has her own life to lead? But in which direction is it leading her? That's what I'm concerned about. Towards a lonely old age in a rented room in Kentish Town?

Last week I saw a bag-lady in Hendon. She had uncombed grey hair and filthy clothes, and she was muttering obscenities left and right as she dragged some poor flea-bitten dog along on a lead. As I crossed the road to avoid her, I said to myself: There goes my Sharon in a few years' time. Because if Sharon doesn't start looking for a husband soon, I don't see what decent future is left for her.

But wait a minute! Perhaps she does want to get married! But perhaps after so many years with so little luck in the marriage stakes, she has relinquished all hope of being a bride. After all, it can't be pleasant seeing your contemporaries from school get married and settle down when you're still single, and she's such a proud girl. Maybe she has lost confidence in her prospects. Poor darling, she will get married, of course she will. She's really very beautiful – or would be, if she took more care with her appearance. As I told her when she and Robert came to dinner last Friday night, 'When a woman gets to her thirties, she can no longer just throw on a pair of jeans and rely on her natural beauty to get her by. She needs a little artifice.'

'You're right, Mum,' she said, smirking across the table at Robert. 'I'd better buy myself a wig and a mask – and perhaps a fan I can hide my wrinkles behind.'

'You may well be facetious,' I said. 'But you ought to listen to me. Shouldn't she, Robert?' And without waiting for him to disagree with me I went on, 'One day, Sharon, when you're old and alone and it's too late to do anything about it, you'll realize you should have taken my advice and you'll be very, very sorry.'

At which she lost her temper in the sudden way she

often does with me, flaring up like a box of matches on fire. 'You'd love that, wouldn't you, Mum? In fact, you just can't wait to say "I told you so"!'

'Don't be silly,' I said. 'I hope I never have to. I hope my most dreadful worries don't come true. And if they do, Please God I'm not still around to see it happen.'

'Why? Where will you be?' she shouted. 'Up in that great marriage bureau in the sky?' And having said this, she stormed out of the room, slamming the door so hard that the noise even made Morry look up from his newspaper.

'What's the matter?' he said, squinting at me reproach-fully through his reading-glasses. 'Not another row?'

'Yes, another row!' I said. 'You'd know that yourself if you'd lifted your eyes from that paper! Why, you've been reading throughout the meal!'

He looked bewildered. 'I'm not reading,' he said in a hurt voice. 'I'm doing the crossword.'

Which upset me so much that I burst into tears. 'Don't cry, Mum,' Robert said, getting up from his chair, and putting his arms around me from behind.

'I can't help it, darling,' I wept. 'Watching Sharon ruin her life is breaking my heart. Believe me, I only want the best for her. For both of you,' I added after a short pause. 'To see you both happy and settled. Now is that too much to ask?'

'Sometimes it is,' he mumbled.

'Why?' I asked, on the spur of the moment. But the second I'd said it, I regretted it, because his hands froze where they were on my shoulders. There was a tense silence.

'Because –' he began. Then he stopped suddenly, and turning on his heel, walked out of the room.

I looked at Morry, who had folded up his newspaper and was glaring at me furiously. 'For God's sake, leave that boy alone!' he shouted. 'Leave them both alone, Gloria! They'll either get married or they won't – all in their own good time!'

'What do you mean, "in their own good time"?' I retorted. 'We've let them do it "in their own good time" so far, and look what's happened – absolutely nothing! How long do we wait before we intervene?'

'As long as it bloody takes!' he yelled, pushing back his chair and following in Robert's wake.

The door swung shut behind him, and I was left alone in the silent dining-room. I gazed blankly at the remnants of the meal: the half-drunk bottle of wine; the white Sabbath candles burning in my grandmother's silver candlesticks; the cut-glass bowl of coleslaw; the congealing latkes; the abandoned plates of half-eaten plaice fillets and semi-demolished gefilte fish-balls I had spent hours chopping and frying with love. My heart sank. Not again, I said to myself. I mean, why must every painstakingly prepared Friday-night dinner end in a row? No wonder Morry suffers so from indigestion and heartburn, with all the shouting and running about! The children come for dinner so seldom – so why can't these occasions be pleasant? Morry blames me for the arguments, I know he does. But what have I done? Is it wrong to want the best for your children? I hardly dare say a word of what I think to either of them any more. How come they feel they can say what they want to me, but I'm not allowed to open my mouth?

I must concentrate.

. . . nothing is as lasting and as fulfilling for a woman

as a good, solid, happy marriage founded on mutual respect, honesty and love . . .

I don't think I can carry on writing today.

Thursday, 16th October

I have been thinking about what I was thinking about Sharon yesterday. Perhaps Morry is right and I do worry about her too much. After all, what is the worry when there have never been any spinsters in our family? Even my grandmother's sister May, who had sticking-out teeth and was simple in the head, found herself a man – that is to say, the family found one for her. It is true that Ivor, God rest his soul, had bad breath and remained a *shlepper* at Angel Dresses all his life, and so could never be considered Sharon's 'type', but nevertheless May was happy enough with him.

But what is Sharon's 'type'? I'm blowed if I know. Somehow I can't see her settling for an Ivor. If she wasn't so fussy, she might have got married long ago. But she's always turned her nose up at decent boys, as long ago as I can remember. Why, when she was fifteen and starting to go to parties, extremely nice young men would come to the house to escort her. But after one, or at the most two dates, they would stop coming and their names would never be uttered again. If I happened to make a remark like, 'What's happened to So-and-so? He was such a nice fellow,' she'd scowl at me and say, 'Mum, he was revolting!' to which I'd reply innocuously, 'Don't be silly, dear, he was just the sort you ought to hang your hat up with,' and she'd shout back rudely, 'Why don't you mind your own business and leave me alone?'

It's 7.15 now, and time to get down to Chapter Three.

Where did I leave off yesterday? With a marriage founded on 'mutual respect, honesty and love'. Which is the kind of relationship I have with dear Morry. First of all, we respect each other, the way we each are and all the things we do. I mean, I respect everything about my husband – everything except his mania for reading. And I know he respects me, even though he said yesterday that my Hoovering the garden path was 'crass stupidity'.

Naturally we both believe in being honest with one another. As husband and wife, we tell each other everything. Well, almost everything – there's no point in being too honest, I feel, especially when you know that if you tell the truth you're going to hurt someone. For instance, there's no point in telling Morry of my worries about Robert, is there, when he'd only drop dead of a heart attack right away? No, in my opinion there is a time and a place for honesty. When and where that time and place are I have yet to discover. I only know they're not at the dinner table, when Morry remarks that the soup I've spent all afternoon preparing is too salty, nor when he sees me in the bath and remarks that my spare tyre has grown. In my humble opinion, that kind of 'honesty' is nothing but cruelty.

As for love – well, of course Morry and I love each other dearly, and have done since the day we met at a charity ball. I remember it well, as our eyes fused across the dance-floor . . . Hold on a moment, this bit ought to be in my book.

The September night was warm, and I was wearing a delightful off-the-shoulder blue-moiré dress with green trim around the edges. As my friend Claudia and I swept into the hall, my eyes immediately fused with those of a tall, handsome, dark-haired man who was standing on the far side of the dance-floor, not far from the band.

'Who is that?' I whispered, leaning close to Claudia.'

Her eyes lit up. 'Why, don't you know?' she said. 'That's Morris Gold, the brilliant up-and-coming entrepreneur.'

What will Christian think of this? It sounds rather like the new story Melanie Thatcher read out in class last night, which is full of women 'sweeping' in and out of rooms, being 'washed over' with emotion, and 'mopping' their love-fevered brows – almost the vocabulary I'd use to describe what I do in the kitchen, as I said when it was my turn to criticize it. This made Christian laugh for the only time during the evening – he has been looking very glum lately, I must say. I think he has lost the enthusiasm for teaching he had at the beginning of term. In fact, he was extremely nasty about Melanie's style. However, she seemed to have forgiven him by the end of the class, because when they went off to the pub together she was looking very cheerful indeed.

Does Christian's wife mind him going out till all hours drinking with strange women? I wonder if he might be a bit of a philanderer. Thank God this kind of thing is not something I have to worry about with Morry, who is as faithful as I am. I can't imagine him making advances to anyone. Even to me. Though I don't often think about these things, it's suddenly occurred to me that I cannot remember the last time we 'made love'. Not that this is important – when you get to our age, you couldn't care less. That is, unless you're someone like my mother, but then the least said the better about her and the way she still flirts, even with bus conductors . . . The way she always flirted, right under my darling father's nose . . .

Oh dear, I can't bear to think about the pain she must have caused him. Thank goodness I'm not like she is. No wonder Nanny went mad in the end, trying to shield Ruth and me from the way she behaved!

Monday, 20th October

I have just been re-reading the paragraph I wrote on Friday about my first meeting with Morry, and I was surprised to find several discrepancies between what I have written and what I now remember of the night. For a start, the night was not warm but so cold that my bare arms had turned blue before I had left home. Second, Claudia and I did not 'sweep into the hall' together – she walked ahead, laughing on the arms of both our escorts, and I followed behind on my own, clutching my mother's squirrel stole. As I walked down the entrance steps the stole slipped, one of the squirrel-tails caught under my shoe, and I went stumbling forward on to the dance-floor, where I ended up on my hands and knees with a laddered stocking.

'Oh, well done, Gloria!' Claudia exclaimed, clapping her hands.

'Are you all right?' my escort asked me as he helped me up.

'Perfectly, thank you,' I replied, brushing some dirt off my skirt and hoping that my blush would fade before Claudia noticed it. I remember thinking that in the first minute of being at the ball I had transgressed Nanny's primary rule of social conduct – never to draw attention to oneself in public – and as my escort walked me over to the bar, I wanted to die, I really did, what with everyone turning round and staring at me and giggling. I had been looking forward to the evening for weeks, and now, almost before it had begun, I had ruined it by my own clumsiness. However, the next moment someone coughed behind me and said, 'Excuse me, could I have the next dance?'

I turned round, and there stood a tall, thin young man in an ill-fitting hired dinner-jacket with worn lapels. I took in his sandy-brown hair, his narrow face with hollow cheeks, his rather beaky nose and his twinkling, friendly brown eyes, and suddenly I felt better. 'Certainly,' I said. And added with a laugh, 'If you're brave enough to risk being tripped up.'

'I'd be delighted to fall,' he said, with a grin. Which I have to say made me blush all the deeper, especially when I saw Claudia's surprised expression.

'That was quite an entrance,' he said as he steered me into a clearing among the dancers, the heat of his hand warming the small of my back.

'I'm glad you liked it,' I quipped. 'I've been practising for weeks.'

Apparently, so Morry told me later, it was love at first sight for him, just like it used to be in the movies. For me, love came more slowly. But from the start, something was different with Morry: he was fun to be with; we were relaxed together; I never felt intimidated by him, like I did by Claudia and her rich, clever friends. And even though he had just been demobbed, and was starting out in business by himself and so had little money to spend on posh restaurants and night-clubs, we always had a good time when we went out. Before long he took me home to Hackney to meet his family and then we became engaged.

What I have just set down is the real version of how I met Morry. Though it is completely true, and even brings a lump to my throat when I read it, I know that it is never the sort of thing that one could put in a book, or read out in writing class. For a start, it is too boring, and casts me, the heroine, in too unfavourable a light. I mean, it's bad enough being a *klutz* without telling the world about it. So perhaps I shall use the first version in my book. Whatever the means, the end is the same, isn't it? To say that Morry and I love each other, very, very much.

Perhaps 'very much' would be more appropriate, when I think about it. I mean, after nearly thirty-six years of marriage . . . Let me write it down again: Morry and I love each other very much. Perhaps I should simply say, Morry and I love each other? Or, Morry and I . . .?

I have now been writing for forty-five minutes. Surely that is long enough? After all, I don't want to overdo my commitment to this autobiography. I am still first and foremost a housewife. And it is Monday, and I have a million things to clean around the house. And after lunch I would like to take the bus up to town and drop into Angel Dresses, because I haven't seen Ruth for days.

Besides, thinking about Aunt May and Ivor last week gave me a little idea that just might be the answer to Sharon's problem: I hear Mark's taken on a nice new salesman there.

Tuesday, 21st October

A most disturbing thing happened yesterday while I was up at Angel Dresses, and I'm not sure what I should do about it.

I really feel I ought to do something. I can't just ignore what I overheard. However, when I said this to Morry at supper last night, he said I can and should ignore it, because probably nothing at all is going on, or, if it is, it's only going on in my head. 'As usual,' he concluded.

'What do you mean, as usual?' I said as I dished him out another slice of Wiener schnitzel.

'Gloria,' he sighed, 'you're always worrying. I've never known a person worry as much as you do. What's this on my plate?'

'What does it look like, darling? A second helping.'

'But I haven't finished my first yet.'

'Take your time. What have we got to hurry for? Only the television.'

'I don't think I want any more now, thank you.'

I looked at him anxiously. 'What's the matter? Don't you like it?'

'It's delicious, but —'

'But?' I interrupted him. 'I suppose it's dry?'

'No, Gloria, it's not dry,' he said patiently, as if he was talking to a child. 'I've just had enough, that's all.'

He put down his knife and fork, wiped his mouth, picked up his biro and filled in a clue in the newspaper crossword. I frowned. 'You call what you just ate enough? You'll fade away if you're not careful.'

'Don't be foolish, Gloria,' he muttered without looking up. 'I'm bursting out of my trousers.'

I looked proudly at the tummy that surged over his waistband. 'That's a healthy sign,' I said, giving it a little pat.

'I'm getting fat,' he said accusingly. 'I can't eat as much as I used to. And I had the most awful indigestion after lunch today.'

'Again? That's the fourth time in a fortnight. I don't understand it – how could three chopped-liver sandwiches and two slices of marble cake give you indigestion? Didn't I pack enough pickled cucumbers to go with the sandwiches? Wasn't the cake moist enough? I don't know, there must be something wrong with you, Morry.'

'There's nothing wrong with me, Gloria. And believe me, it wasn't your sandwiches.'

'How can you be sure?'

'Because I didn't eat them.'

I laughed. 'What did you do with them – polish your shoes?'

He filled in an Across clue and shrugged. 'I fancied something different, that's all. So I gave them to Roy.'

My jaw dropped. 'You gave away the chopped-liver sandwiches I'd made especially for you, and my home-made honey cake, to Roy? To the *shlepper* in your factory?'

'He's not a *shlepper* any more, Gloria. We promoted him to a packer the other week.'

'Mazeltov. If I'd known, I'd have made smoked-salmon sandwiches and slipped in a bottle of champagne.' I drew breath, trying to control my fury. 'I don't mind slaving away for you, Morry, but I do mind doing it for some packer or *shlepper!*' By now, I'm glad to say, he was looking a little shame-faced. 'Why did you do it?' I asked.

'I already told you. I fancied a change. I . . . I went out to eat.'

'Where to?'

'Does it matter?'

'Morry, where to?'

He nose-dived towards the crossword. 'To McDonald's,' he said in a muffled voice.

I gasped. 'How could you? Well, no wonder you had indigestion this afternoon. Let's hope it was indigestion, and not the beginning of something worse. Don't you know that having warm meat hanging around for hours in buns is just the time when salmonella germs develop? Perhaps I'd better call Dr Sheiner . . .'

'Stop it, Gloria!' he shouted, grabbing my wrist as I made for the phone and pulling me back down on to my chair. 'How many times do I have to tell you, eating a hamburger is perfectly safe! Millions of people eat them every day.'

'But you said yourself it gave you pains!'

'Gloria, Gloria!' he sighed. 'Here you go again! It's like I said before, you're always worrying about something. At breakfast today you were worried that Sharon might be mugged on the Underground, when you called me at work this morning you were worried in case Robert's cleaning lady gave him the flu. Now it's salmonella poisoning. A few minutes ago it was your sister and her husband.'

'That's different.'

'It's always "different" – every time.'

'No, it's really different. I mean it, Morry.'

'Yes, yes, I know, Gloria. You always do. What do you have to go on? A few words you thought you overheard? Shame on you for eavesdropping!'

'I was not eavesdropping. My hands were full, and I couldn't open the door, that's why I was standing outside it. And I did not think I overheard Mark – I did overhear him.'

I did, I did. Though I admit my imagination carries me away at times, it was not working at that particular instant when I was standing outside the door to the small private office with a cup of coffee in one hand, an order book in the other, and a handbag strap in danger of sliding off my shoulder. What was on my mind was this: How can I open the door without spilling coffee all over me? I leaned against the door for a moment, wondering how best I could accomplish this. I thought of calling out for someone to help me, but there was no one in the corridor, and from what I could hear, there was no one in the little office either because there was silence inside.

Suddenly, the silence broke, and I heard a scuffle. Then

a woman's voice murmured, 'What are we going to do?'

What was I going to do, that was what concerned me. I was about to give the door a kick to attract the attention of whoever-it-was when another voice said, 'I really don't know. Things can't go on like this much longer.'

That was Mark's voice. I froze where I was out of natural curiosity, even though the coffee was by now burning my fingers through the thin plastic cup, and I pressed my ear closer to the door.

'No, they can't,' the first voice said. The tone was a woman's, high, breathy, not unfamiliar. 'We'll have to tell her soon,' she continued. I heard Mark swear under his breath. 'We've got to,' the woman went on. 'If we don't, she'll see for herself, and everything will be ruined.'

Then Mark mumbled something I couldn't properly hear. And then, damn it, my shoulder-strap slipped, my bag plummeted on to my elbow, and the coffee went flying everywhere. 'Oh blast!' I shrieked before I could stop myself. A second later the office door was flung open, and I practically fell into Mark's arms. For a second his piercing blue eyes betrayed suspicion and apprehension, and then his face broke into its usual, devastating smile.

'Whoops!' he laughed as he rescued the order book and my coat from my coffee-drenched hands. 'Done it again, Gloria, have you?'

'Oh, you know me,' I said. 'Such a clumsy old thing.' I looked around: the new designer, Hattie, was sitting at the desk, smoothing her tangled blonde hair, and gazing intently at some sketches that were spread out before her.

'Hallo Mrs Gold,' she said, looking up at me and giving me a small quick smile, which I must say did nothing to hide the guilty look in her eyes.

I took in her pinched cheeks and her smudged,

shocking-pink lipstick. 'Hallo Hattie,' I said coldly, putting my bag on the chair beside her, taking a tissue from the box on the desk and mopping dry my hands.

'Oh no, just look at your skirt!' she exclaimed as I sat down. 'You've got coffee all over it! Here, let me get a damp towel to sponge it down.' She jumped up and started to squeeze past me, and I was treated to a whiff of a strong heady perfume.

'Don't trouble yourself,' I said firmly. 'It's Polyester. The stains will come out in the wash.'

'Are you sure?'

Mark grinned. 'If there's one thing my sister-in-law is sure of, it's how to get things clean. Isn't that so, Gloria?'

I gave him a half-smile. We then lapsed into an uneasy silence, Mark lounging in the doorway, Hattie hesitating behind my chair. And I suddenly got the most uncomfortable feeling that, instead of being in the office of the family business, a place I have always looked on as a second home, I was an unwanted intruder in a strange place.

'Excuse me, I must see if Lucy has finished cutting out my sample,' Hattie said eventually, and pushed under Mark's upstretched arm and out of the door with her head lowered. Mark cleared his throat.

'I hope I haven't interrupted an important discussion,' I said to him.

'Of course not,' he said, rather too quickly for me to believe it was true. 'Well, not really,' he added. 'We were just deciding what to do about Marika, the new machinist. I don't know where Ruth found her, but the bloody woman can't sew a straight seam. Half of Hattie's samples have come out twisted and puckered. It's a bit worrying when we've got the mid-season show coming up soon.'

I breathed a sigh of relief – so that explained what I

had heard through the door about 'having to tell her', and things being ruined. Or so I thought at the time. But a few minutes later, when Ruth joined me in the office and Mark went out, I happened to say that I'd heard she was having trouble with her new sample machinist and she looked at me as if I was mad.

'Whatever gave you that idea?' she said. 'Marika's terrific. In fact, she's one of the most skilled workers I've had in a long time.'

'Oh. I thought Mark said . . .' I shrugged. 'I must have been mistaken.'

'Yes, you must,' Ruth snapped.

Which is just what Morry concluded last night when I told him my suspicions about Mark and Hattie.

'I don't know a happier couple than Ruth and Mark,' he insisted. 'Look how well they get on together – and they're in each other's company twenty-four hours a day. Can you imagine us doing that?'

Which I have to say upset me more than ever. Because when I thought about it at one-thirty this morning as I lay awake and sleepless in bed, I frankly could not imagine Morry and I doing that. Why, we run out of things to say to each other at breakfast!

Talking of which . . . It is five to eight, my writing hour is all but over, and I haven't written a word of Chapter Three. Whatever happened to my resolution not to be distracted?

Should I tell Ruth what I suspect? Morry says that to do so would be 'unforgivable meddling'. If I mention it to Angel, she'd only tell Ruth. And what is there to tell? That I overheard a snatch of conversation that could have been about anything? Yet if I don't mention it to Ruth and something dreadful happens, I'll feel terrible. No wonder I'm worried. Oh, what should I do?

Thursday, 23rd October

All thoughts of Mark and Ruth were swept from my mind during last night's class. Because who would have believed what a filthy mind was hidden inside that sweet old Mrs Balgrove? I mean, when she said at the beginning of term that she had had some short stories published, even Christian had no idea they were 'spanking' stories for specialized pornographic magazines. When she read us her latest opus before tea-break I was hard-pressed to keep a straight face – and so I think were the other students. I have to say that Christian behaved like a real gentleman: he criticized the story seriously when she had finished reading it, and said it was an interesting example of the pure erotic genre. There seemed nothing pure about it to me. How does she think of all those variations? She must have a very lurid imagination. Unless, that is, she knows such things from her own experience. Might she have done them in her youth, with her late husband? Ugh! I don't want to think about it! And yet, oh dear, I've just had a vision of a toothless old man tying Mrs B to a bedpost and lashing her with her thick crêpe stockings! Oh, God help me, I'm starting to laugh!

Oh heavens, that feels better. I don't think I've laughed like that for weeks. As I told Christian when we were standing in the coffee-queue, creative writing is turning out to be much more serious than I'd anticipated.

'Well, it can be a depressing business,' he said. 'Nevertheless, Gloria, I think you should try to give your autobiography a light touch. Remember, writers must be able to laugh at themselves. But I'm sure you do that anyway. Unless,' he added with a sly smile, 'you see yourself as a victim of domestic tragedy?'

83

'Not at all,' I protested. 'As a matter of fact, I'm an extremely happy woman. Why, with two wonderful children, and such a nice husband, what woman couldn't be happy?' But when his wide-spaced green eyes met mine, I realized that he didn't believe me, and I was reminded suddenly of a line he'd read out last week, 'The lady doth protest too much, methinks' – and I suddenly felt all funny inside, as if he saw right through me, and what he saw was that I wasn't happy at all. Feeling thoroughly confused, I turned away and reached out for a slice of fruit cake.

'So, what did you think of Mrs Balgrove's story?' he confided as we carried our cups towards a table.

'Well . . .' I faltered, not wanting him to think me small-minded. 'I mean . . . it was . . . very, um, interesting.'

'Yes, very interesting indeed.' I glanced at him, and saw that he was grinning at me. 'It turns out she's quite a girl,' he went on. 'It just goes to show, doesn't it?'

'To show what?' I said. Then, 'That you can't judge a book by its cover,' we said in unison, and started to laugh, which dispelled the awkwardness between us.

'Actually, talking of covers, there's something I wanted to ask you,' I said tentatively as we sat down at an empty table. 'You're a published author. You know about these things. Must one have a photograph on the cover of one's autobiography? You see, I'm not terribly photogenic.'

'Ah, Gloria,' he exclaimed. 'Does this mean you've nearly finished it?'

I hesitated. 'Um, well, no, not exactly.'

'But you've made a good start?'

'Sort of. Well . . .'

'Mind if we join you?' said Irene, plonking her coffee down next to Christian's.

84

Melanie sat down opposite us and simpered across at Christian. 'Don't let us disturb you,' she breathed.

Christian glanced at me, hesitating. 'We were just discussing Gloria's autobiography,' he said.

'Oh, let's change the subject,' I said quickly. 'It really doesn't matter.'

However, Christian somehow sensed that it did matter to me, and when the class ended he came up to me and asked if I was still having trouble – as he put it – 'finding the right voice'. When I nodded dismally, he said, 'Well, isn't it time you took a deep breath and brought something in for us to hear?'

I shook my head. 'I just couldn't.'

He smiled sympathetically. 'You know, Gloria, reading work out loud in front of other people isn't easy for anyone here. But it's what gives life and substance to a creative writing class. And you might well find the criticism helpful.'

'You don't understand,' I admitted. 'I've nothing to read out.'

'Nothing at all?'

I shook my head. 'Only a few pages.'

'Oh dear,' he said. 'You are having problems. Would you like to talk about it in a smaller group? How about coming to the pub for a drink?'

'Thank you, but I never go to pubs,' I said quickly. And in case that seemed rude, I added in explanation, 'It's because I'm Jewish.'

At this he roared with laughter. 'I didn't know entering pubs was against your religion!'

I laughed too. Was his humour infectious, or was I beginning to understand what he'd said before about not taking yourself too seriously? 'You know what I mean,' I muttered. 'We Jews don't drink very much. Well, not in pubs. Not usually.'

'Well, how about breaking with the tradition?'

I shook my head and clutched my handbag tightly. 'I couldn't,' I said. 'You see, my husband's expecting me home.'

'Now, Gloria, that's an even worse excuse!'

By this time, the classroom had almost emptied, and Irene, Melanie, Gerrard and Dr Seal were waiting impatiently for Christian outside the open door. 'Hurry up, Chris!' Irene called. 'It'll be last orders at the bar soon.'

'Go ahead,' he said. 'I'll see you there in a moment.' He turned off the light switches, plunging the classroom into darkness. 'What am I going to do with you, Gloria?' he said as we walked slowly down the empty corridor. 'You can't talk about your writing in class, you won't talk about it anywhere else.' He sighed. 'Still, somehow I feel you're capable of doing some good work.'

'What on earth makes you think that?' I asked with genuine curiosity.

He shrugged. 'You certainly seem to have the commitment. You try hard enough. Anyway, I'm reluctant to give up on you just yet. Look, perhaps you and I could meet outside class one day and look at whatever you've done?'

'I couldn't possibly ask you to give up your spare time!' I said. 'Why, a real novelist like you must have a hundred more important things to do than talk to an amateur like me!'

All of a sudden his face took on the gloomy look it has often had in the last few weeks. 'As a matter of fact, I'm at rather a loose end at the moment,' he confided in a low voice. 'I'm a bit stuck with my work and . . . Truthfully,

I'd be rather glad of something to occupy myself. Look, how about meeting me tomorrow for lunch?'

And so, in a few hours' time I'm meeting him at Golders Green station. He's expecting me to bring all the little scraps I've written with me so we can discuss them. What on earth shall I take?

I've just come back from Golders Green and although I know I ought to do the cleaning I didn't have time for this morning because the house is really in an awful mess, I'm so excited that I couldn't possibly wait until tomorrow to write down what happened. I must do it right away.

Christian and I had arranged to meet at Golders Green station, so I went by car, and parked in a side-street. As I walked into the main road, who should I see but my mother, wheeling her shopping basket straight towards me, her slender body swamped beneath her old mink coat, her immaculate lilac hair secured under a leopard-printed head-scarf.

'Gloria!' she exclaimed.

'Oh, hallo Mummy. How lovely to see you,' I said with horror.

'It's a small world, isn't it?' she said, resting the wheeler on its metal haunches as if she was expecting us to have a long chat.

'Yes, it is,' I agreed. As I looked over her shoulder, I caught sight of Christian standing in the bus station in his baggy tweed jacket, and I wished suddenly that I'd arranged to meet him in Hampstead or Kilburn or Oxford Street – anywhere, in fact, that wasn't Golders Green. I should have known I'd be bound to bump into someone who knew me. Given my luck, it had to be Angel.

She did what she always does when she first sees me – gave me the once-over from head to toe to see if I was 'properly' dressed. 'Is that overcoat the one you bought three years ago in D. H. Evans' sale?'

'Yes, it's lasted well, hasn't it?' I said proudly. Then added with a sinking feeling, 'Why? What's wrong with it?'

'Nothing's wrong with it,' she said in a voice that assured me that there certainly was. 'I'm sure it was a very smart coat in its day. But, Gloria, hemlines are up this year. And look, there's a thread hanging from the sleeve.' So saying she lifted my arm to her vividly-painted lips, and bit the thread off with her teeth.

There went my confidence, chewed off by Angel's dentures and thrown on the ground. For the millionth time in my life, I cursed having a mother who was a dress designer. People used to envy me her when I was young. But if they had known what it was like, always to have one's appearance the subject of professional scrutiny, they might have envied me less.

'You might have told me you were coming here this morning, and offered me a lift,' she continued in a disgruntled voice. 'I had to wait hours for the bus. What brings you here? A hairdresser's appointment?'

The last shreds of my confidence disintegrated. 'I'm meeting someone for lunch,' I said.

Her cheeks lifted even higher than they had after her last face-lift as she broke into a delighted smile. 'Oh good. In that case I'll join you. I'm dying for something to eat.'

'Oh, no I . . . No, I don't think . . .' To my horror, I found myself tongue-tied. Because for some strange reason, I didn't want to tell her I was having lunch with Christian. 'I'm afraid it isn't convenient,' I stuttered.

She drew herself up to her full height of five foot one inch, an action which, though I'm a good three inches taller than she is, is always guaranteed to make me feel small. 'I get the message,' she said curtly. 'You don't want my company. You're ashamed of me. Well, Gloria, thank God your dear father isn't alive to see this day!'

Naturally, this made me feel terrible. 'Of course I'm not ashamed of you,' I protested. 'It's just that . . . just that . . .'

'Spit it out, for heaven's sake.' Over her shoulder, across in the station, I caught sight of Christian again. Angel's eyes narrowed. 'Gloria, you're turning red.'

'Am I?' My hands flew to my burning cheeks. 'Heavens, it must be the wind. Look, Mummy,' I went on, gathering my thoughts together. 'It's a bit delicate. You see, I'm, er . . . I'm meeting a woman from my synagogue. She's having trouble with her husband, who's being rather difficult. She wants to discuss him with me.'

She raised her pencilled-in eyebrows. 'What could you possibly know about difficult husbands? Oh well, in that case, I'm off to have a sandwich by myself. I'm not going to stand here all day in the cold, catching my death. And the wind is extremely bad for the complexion, you know. Talking of which, I think you ought to change your foundation, Gloria. A touch more beige would do wonders to take that ruddiness away.'

When Christian asked me where I wanted to go for lunch, I tried to think where we were least likely to bump into Angel. 'Um, there's a nice pub round the corner,' I suggested.

'Gloria Gold,' he exclaimed. 'I thought it was against your religion!'

'Well,' I quipped, 'a woman's got to break with tradition some day.'

Once we were seated in the pub, I had something else to worry about: we had come there to talk about my writing; so what was I going to say? But before I could say anything, I noticed that Christian himself was looking so terribly glum that I simply had to ask him what the matter was. The consequence was that we never got to talk about my autobiography at all.

Life is strange and mysterious, isn't it? You never know quite what's going to happen to you, even at my age. I mean, who would have thought a few weeks ago, when I was an ordinary housewife cleaning the hall carpet, that my decision to write a book would lead to this? That I, Gloria Gold, would soon become the confidante of a real published novelist! It is as hard to believe as it is to believe that Christian's second wife would run off and leave him two weeks ago, leaving no forwarding address and, besides and even worse to my mind, nothing in the fridge.

'Didn't she even make sure there was something for your supper — say, just a loaf of bread and a piece of cheese?'

He shook his head. 'Nothing at all.'

I drew myself up. 'Well!'

'Do you really think that's so bad, Gloria?'

'I think it's terrible!'

'Yes,' he sighed. 'I suppose it is. But you see, that's typical of how she's been throughout our marriage. She's not what you would call the housewife type.'

My hackles rose. 'Ah,' I said with growing hostility. 'She's a career woman?'

He nodded again, and gazed into his pint of bitter. 'How did you know?'

'I know the type,' I said. And then confided, 'I have one in my family. My daughter Sharon . . .' I sighed, as I seem to do whenever I think about her. 'But don't let me bore you with my own problems.'

He looked up from his beer with raised eyebrows. 'I thought you didn't have any problems.'

'Well, they aren't real problems as such,' I lied, and, clearing my throat, quickly changed the subject. 'Um, if you don't mind my asking, why has your wife left you?'

He shrugged. 'I guess she's had enough. It's not much fun being married to a writer.'

It's not much fun being married to someone in the rag-trade either, I thought to myself. I mean, coming home all covered in dust from heaving all those dress-rails about, and then being so exhausted all he can do is bloody read! And then I realized what I was thinking and felt quite shocked. Why had I had such a disloyal thought all of a sudden? What was the matter with me?

'I suppose she just got fed up with me,' Christian continued in a mournful tone. He frowned, pushed back his untidy hair, and leaned his leather elbow-patch in a spilled puddle of beer. 'Fed up with my lack of success. I can't blame her. After all, I'm forty-six, and what have I done with my life? I've been married twice, and both times have been failures. I've got two teenage kids by my first wife I pay through the nose for and never see. I haven't lived up to Caroline's expectations.'

'But marriage isn't about living up to expectations,' I protested.

'Isn't it? What else is it about?'

'Well . . .' Suddenly my mind went blank. What *was* marriage about when I came to think of it? At last, in desperation, I thought of what I'd written in my autobiography. 'Why, it's about support and friendship and . . . why, and mutual understanding. It's about sticking by a person through thick and thin. Anyway you're a successful, respected author, Christian! That's something for her to be proud of.'

'I'm not successful enough, and not respected,' he mumbled.

'What does she want? That you should be another Shakespeare? To tell you the truth, I've never liked his plays much. They're so hard to follow. Why use ten words when one will do?'

When I said this he threw back his head and laughed as if I'd made the most tremendous joke, and said I was a real joy to be with, a breath of fresh air in a world gone sour, and it had cheered him up no end to have lunch with me. Well, whether he meant it or not, it certainly makes a change to be called a breath of fresh air instead of an old nagger – which is what Morry called me when I came home from class last night to find him sitting on the sofa watching TV with his feet up on the footstool and a chicken drumstick in his hand.

'Morry,' I said. 'Is this some kind of protest because I've been to my evening class?'

'Not at all,' he muttered with his mouth full. 'As far as I'm concerned, you can go out every night.'

'Where's your plate? Don't tell me you haven't got one? Honestly, you'll get grease everywhere!'

'Don't be such an old nagger! Why make such a production over a little nosh?'

'Because there's no need to eat on the living-room furniture! What's got into you? And – Good God, Morry, I don't believe it! You've taken the dust covers off some of the cushions! Why on earth?'

'Because, Gloria,' he snapped. 'For a short period while you were out, I was trying to pretend that I was living in a normal home!'

I sat down on the armchair, folded my arms tightly and nursed my hurt. 'Well,' I said eventually. 'How was the goulash I left in the oven?'

'Fine,' he murmured without expression. Then, 'Actually, I didn't eat it.'

'Why not?'

'I didn't fancy it. I had a touch of heartburn this afternoon.'

'Not again? I know – you went to McDonald's for lunch, didn't you? Don't deny it, Morry. Well, no wonder you had heartburn! Believe me, if God had meant Jews to eat hamburgers, he'd have given them a more kosher name!'

It's five o'clock now, so I'd better stop writing and start cooking tonight's dinner. Somehow my elation has disappeared in the course of writing all this down. Oh well. I wonder what Christian is going to eat for his supper tonight? Perhaps I should have asked him over? On second thoughts, I can't imagine him sitting here with me and Morry.

I wonder why his second wife got fed up with him. Could it really have been because their marriage wasn't any fun? Marriage fun? What an idea!

Friday, 24th October

My marriage to Morry . . .

Oh my God, the telephone is ringing! And it's only five past seven! In my experience, a call this early in the morning can only mean one thing: something awful has happened to someone in the family. I feel sick, I hardly dare answer it . . .

I did answer it. And as I suspected something terrible has happened – the thing I've been secretly dreading since I went to the showroom on Monday. This'll teach Morry to tell me I worry about nothing. I should never have listened to him. If only I'd been more vigilant in my anxiety, nothing at all might have happened. But let go of a worry and there's a 99 per cent chance it'll creep up behind you and thump you on the head even harder than you expected it to, just to say 'I told you so'.

When I picked up the phone I heard a woman crying on the other end of the line. 'Gloria,' she sobbed.

'Ruth?'

'Oh, Gloria!'

By the way those sobs were coming from the pit of her stomach, I could tell that something dreadful had happened. As I sank down on Sharon's old bed, all the awful things that could be wrong ran through my head, making me dizzy with fear. 'Darling, what's the matter?'

'Oh Gloria!' she cried again.

My heart contracted. 'It's Mummy, isn't it?' I guessed.

A sob caught in her throat. 'Mummy!' she wailed.

Tears sprang to my eyes for the loss of Angel. 'Don't say another word. Oh my God, Ruth, Mummy's dead!'

'Mummy's dead!' she shrieked. 'Oh, Gloria, no! I can't believe it! Not this! When did it happen?'

I stopped crying for a moment. 'What do you mean, when? Last night, I suppose.'

'Last night!' Her crying was reaching a frenzy. 'Oh God, Gloria! Darling Angel? How did you find out?'

'What do you mean, how?' I sobbed. 'You just told me!'

Her crying stopped. 'How could I, when I didn't know?'

'Of course you knew. You rang to tell me!'

'No, I didn't. I didn't know anything about it until you told me just now. Oh God, I just can't carry on! Not with this as well! Oh, poor Mummy!'

'But . . .' I blew my nose. 'I only said she was dead

because that's what I thought you were phoning to say. I –'

'Oh, for God's sake!' she interrupted angrily. 'Stop messing about. Tell me straight – is Mummy dead or not?'

Again I hesitated. 'Well, I haven't heard anything if you haven't,' I murmured.

'Thank God!' she gasped.

'What a blessing!' I sighed with relief. 'I mean, she was looking healthy enough when I bumped into her yesterday. A little tired, perhaps, but –' I broke off as I realized Ruth had started crying again. 'Well, what is the matter if it's not Mummy, darling?'

'It's Mark,' she whispered. Fresh tears sprang to my eyes with the realization that my baby sister was probably a widow. 'He . . . he didn't come home last night.'

My blood ran cold. 'Have you phoned the police?' I asked in a voice of icy calm. 'Have you checked the hospitals? Don't panic yet, Ruth, because for all you know he may still be alive.'

'He is alive. He's just phoned me,' she wept on in a surprisingly bitter tone.

'Thank God! Why didn't he ring you sooner? Did he have an accident?'

Ruth blew her nose. 'No, he didn't. He's just gone.'

'Gone where?' I said.

'Just gone. Don't you understand? He's left me, Gloria. He's run off with Hattie.'

Suddenly the meaning of the conversation I had over-heard in the showroom on Monday became all too clear to me. 'Oh no! Ruth, darling, no!'

'Yes! And not only that,' she went on, her voice ascending towards hysteria. 'There's worse. He . . . he phoned me from some new showroom they've hired in Mortimer

Street. It seems that they intend to set up in business together. As rivals to Angel Dresses. Manufacturing evening dresses, just like we do. And they've . . . they've taken the new mid-season collection with them. And all the patterns, so I can't cut any new samples.'

'But they can't,' I said. 'I mean, how can they?'

'My collection, Gloria. They've stolen my mid-season samples! All my best designs! This whole thing must have been going on right under my nose! I could die when I think of it. How could I not have seen it? Oh, Gloria, I feel so humiliated. I can't face going to the office. What the hell am I going to say to everyone? And what am I going to do?'

It's now midday, I have just come back from the show-room, and all I can say is, am I glad to be home! What with Mummy and Ruth both in top gear, I hardly got a word in edgeways, and when I did, I was jumped on immediately. Not that I can blame them. Poor Ruth and poor Mummy and poor all-the-people-who-work-there. Because Mark and Hattie really have taken all the best mid-season samples to their new showroom.

'All they've left us with are these!' Ruth said tearfully, sorting roughly through some limp jersey dresses hanging on the one remaining rail. 'All the lousy *shmutters* that *she* made!'

'Terrible,' Mummy said, examining one of them. 'I always said that girl couldn't cut a straight seam. College trained! Look – this even has bust darts! Why, no one uses bust darts in this day and age!'

Here Ruth slumped down on one of the showroom chairs, and put her head in her hands. 'Oh God,' she moaned. 'I just can't believe this is happening. What am I going to do?'

'Put some make-up on for a start,' Angel said crisply. 'Once you've got some rouge on those cheeks, life will begin to look brighter again. You look absolutely terrible.'

'Yes, you do, darling,' I chimed in in a concerned voice, more worried than I dared express by Ruth's appearance. Because somehow overnight her face had lost all its former softness – now it looked hard and old. Her eyes were red and baggy and underlined with deep shadows, and her lovely cupid-lips were bitten quite raw. 'What if some customers came in?' I went on gently. 'You couldn't serve them looking like that.'

She looked up at me with blazing eyes and I realized that, as usual, I'd managed to say the wrong thing. 'I couldn't serve them anyway,' she snapped bitterly. 'What the fuck have I got left to sell them?'

'Ruth,' I said. 'There's no need to swear.'

'There's every need, as far as I can see,' she said, looking at me in disbelief. 'Jesus, Gloria, my husband's run off with the designer, stealing my best samples and ruining the business Mummy and I have worked for all our lives! You know finances are tight. There's a good chance that without a good season Angel will go under, yet Mark, Mark . . . And you have the bloody nerve to tell me not to swear! Sometimes you're just incredible. Besides, I'm not a child any more. If I want to swear I damn well will, and if you don't like it, well, you can bloody well get out of here!'

'Here, here,' said Angel, looking at me sternly while patting Ruth on the head. 'Ruth's in a crisis. This is no time to play Nanny, Gloria.'

'I was not playing Nanny,' I protested, tears springing to my eyes. 'You're both being unfair. Look, I came round here because I wanted to help. If you don't want me, I'll go home right now. I'm not staying here to be insulted!'

Then Ruth looked a little apologetic, and put her arms around me. 'I'm sorry, Gloria, I didn't mean to take it out on you. I know you mean well. I just don't know what I'm doing today. To think that they've been scheming and planning right under my nose! How can Mark do this? He's my husband! After all these years of working and living together! I thought we were so happy. I mean, he's been a bit distant lately, but I thought . . .'

'Calm yourself,' Mummy said, taking Ruth by the shoulders and drawing herself up into her 'tower-of-strength' pose, the one that she always uses at stone-settings and funerals. 'One must be dignified and keep calm, however bad one feels.' Suddenly she clutched at her pearl necklace, and her voice rose in a hysterical spiral. 'When I think of how your father and I welcomed him into the business all those years ago! A viper in our bosom! The bastard! I'm afraid it's true what they say, girls, one can't trust any man, not even one's husband.'

Coming from Angel, who flirted shamelessly with other men right under Daddy's nose, this was, I felt, a rather bad-taste remark. 'Daddy never betrayed you,' I said pointedly.

Her eyes flashed. 'You don't know everything, Gloria. I said "any man" and I meant it.'

'Even my Morry?'

She sighed. 'Your Morry, as you insist on calling him, isn't a man, he's a saint. Unfortunately, even he can't perform miracles. When he went up to this new show-room of Mark's before, Mark wouldn't even let him through the door.'

'Mark always was a coward,' Ruth wept bitterly. 'He could never face admitting that he'd done wrong. He didn't even have the guts to tell me he was leaving me in person – he had to do it over the telephone.'

There was a moment of quiet, broken only by the sobbing of the machinists next door, with whom Mark had always been a favourite. But then, he was charming, wasn't he? He always had a smile and a good word for everyone. I used to think it was genuine. Now I realize – as the machinists probably did too – that he had us all fooled. He had used Ruth, used Mummy and Daddy, and used Angel Dresses. Now he had no use for them, he was through. 'You know, Ruth,' I said. 'You ought to call your solicitor – maybe even the police.'

She turned white, and glared at me as if I was the one who'd done something wrong. 'I am not calling a lawyer to act against my own husband,' she said. 'And don't tell me what I ought to do. This is between Mark and me, Gloria.'

'Well, if Mark won't talk to Morry, do you think I ought to try and have a word with him?' I asked tentatively.

Angel raised her brows. 'What good could you possibly do? You don't even work here. You don't know anything about the business.'

'No, but I'm his sister-in-law,' I said, rather lamely. Because Mummy was right really, when I come to think about it, why should he listen to his sister-in-law when he wouldn't listen to his wife?

Oh dear, I feel quite overwhelmed with worry. In the face of this, all the other things that have been troubling me lately have quite gone out of my mind. So what that I haven't written a word of my autobiography, or that my darling daughter isn't married, or that there's nothing for dinner because I haven't had time to go shopping yet, or that it's one o'clock and the beds are still unmade, or that my son, my beautiful, wonderful, sweet sweet son hasn't (to my knowledge) ever had a serious girlfriend and for all I know might be . . . be a . . . a . . . and that if he is, he might have that dreadful AI . . .

Good gracious! Thinking of Robert has made me remember something – it's Friday the 24th, and Hannah Cohen's niece Marilyn is coming to dinner tonight! I'd better stop wasting time at this machine and get to the shops before they shut. So what that it's one o'clock and I'm hungry? Where her son's happiness is concerned, any mother worth her salt would only be too glad to go without lunch.

4

The Joys of Motherhood

Sunday, 26th October

The joys of motherhood are multifold. From the moment one leaves the maternity ward with one's darling
little bundle in one's arms, one knows that one has
reached the zenith of happiness . . .

It's no use. I can't write another word. Because after what
Robert told us last night, I simply cannot go on living.
Everything that motivated me before has become empty
and hollow.

I have been a failure as a mother. I should never have
done what I did, and God has set out to punish me
cruelly. Still, do I deserve this? I know I shouldn't have
invited Marilyn for dinner on Friday without asking
Robert first, but I honestly thought it was a good idea at
the time. Believe me, God, all I wanted was some nice
Jewish girl for him to marry. With so many youngsters
marrying out nowadays, I would have thought You'd be
pleased.

She sounded such a nice person when Hannah spoke
about her, the kind of daughter-in-law I've always
dreamed of. How was I to know about her wired jaw?
Couldn't her parents have done something about her

weight problem earlier? Say twenty years ago, when she was in her early teens? As it is, she's thirty-five if she's a day, and thirty-five years haven't been long enough for her to develop what we used to call in my day a 'personality'.

I'll kill Hannah when I next see her. But first of all I'm going to kill myself – if I don't die of a broken heart before I have time to. Perhaps Morry will beat me to it. For all I know, I'll go into the bedroom when I've finished writing this and find him lying there stone dead. How will I manage without him? Oh, Morry, don't leave me here to face this dreadful news of Robert's all alone!

I have just peeked into the bedroom, and thank God, Morry is still snoring like he was when I got up twenty minutes ago. How can a man whose world has recently been shattered by such terrible news sleep so well, that's what I want to know. Why, it's almost indecent!

I had the feeling something shocking was going to happen, ever since Robert rushed off immediately after dinner on Friday leaving Marilyn behind him, saying he had a business appointment to keep. 'At half-past nine on a Friday night?' I shouted from the porch as his BMW sped down the street. The horn honked. That was the last I heard from him for twenty-four hours, until last night when he burst breathlessly into the dining-room while Morry and I were eating supper.

'Look, you two, this can't go on,' he said.

'What can't?' I said.

'This business of introducing me to women. I've told you time and again to stop doing it, but it keeps on happening. I just can't stand it any more.'

'I know it's difficult, Robert,' I said as I dished up the meatballs. 'And I admit Marilyn wasn't all that I'd expected her to be. A boy like you needs someone a little more sophisticated. However one of these days, I'm sure we're going to hit the jackpot. Eat up, Morry.'

'Listen to me –'

'I am listening. And pass the noodles to your father while you're standing there, darling.'

He sat down opposite us and passed the noodles. 'Mum, Dad, there's something we've got to talk about.'

My blood ran cold. Not now, I thought, not after Mark leaving Ruth yesterday, I couldn't stand it. It'll break Morry's heart. 'Have some more sauté potatoes, Morry,' I said.

'Mum, this is important,' Robert insisted. 'We need to talk seriously about . . . about me and women.'

At this, Morry rested his knife and fork on the edge of his plate, closed the book he had been reading and pushed it away. He nodded slowly at Robert, as if he'd been expecting him to say something. 'What is it, son?' he asked, wiping his mouth with his napkin.

Robert gave a quick nervous smile. 'There's something I've got to tell you both. I probably should have told you years ago, but somehow I couldn't bring myself to do it. I . . . I didn't want to hurt you.'

'What's changed?' I mumbled quickly, my mouth full of meatballs. 'Do you want to hurt us now?'

'Of course I don't, Mum. But it's come to the point where not telling you is beginning to hurt me.'

'I see,' I said. The meatball had grown suddenly dry and tasteless. I swallowed it with difficulty. There was a long pause. I glanced at Morry and saw he'd turned as pale as a boiled chicken. When Robert began to speak again, I quickly interrupted him. 'Have a bite to eat, Robert. You're thin as a pin and there's plenty here for all of us –'

At this, Morry rounded on me furiously. 'Will you shut

up, Gloria?' he shouted. 'The boy is trying to tell us something.'

'He can tell us later,' I said tearfully. 'Besides, if it's waited for years, surely it can wait till the end of the meal?'

Morry sighed deeply, and reached for my hand, which he patted gently. 'Gloria, Gloria,' he said, trying to calm me. 'Can't you see this is difficult for Robert? Shut up and let him say what he wants to.'

There was a long silence. Robert started to say something, then changed his mind, got up from the table and walked over to the sideboard. 'There's no point you introducing me to any more women,' he said with his back towards us.

'Oh?'

'You see, it's no use. It's just a farce. Because . . . because . . .' He hesitated for a moment, and then he turned towards us. Never have I seen so much pain on his face – it was quivering under the skin, pulsing in the veins. 'Because I'm not going to take them out, whatever they're like.'

'You don't know that, Robert,' I whispered. 'I mean, if you met the right one . . .'

Morry squeezed my hand. 'Quiet, Gloria.'

Robert looked sadly at me. 'There is no right one, Mum. At least, no right woman. You see, I'm not interested in women. I'm a . . . I'm a homosexual.'

At last he had said it. The word I'd put out of my mind since the first day I'd suspected it echoed in my ears. There was a long silence. Morry put his head in his hands, and I pushed my plate into the centre of the table. Though I had been hungry before the meal, somehow the sight of food now sickened me.

'A homosexual,' I repeated. 'A man who likes men?'

He nodded, then I did too. 'I see. You're telling us you're queer?'

He raised his eyebrows. 'People don't use that expression any more, Mum.'

'Oh?' I said. 'And what do they say?'

'All sorts of names, some of them unpleasant. But we like to call ourselves gay.'

'Gay?' I said. 'There doesn't seem much gaiety about what you're telling me. And who's this "we" you're talking about suddenly?'

He cleared his throat. 'The gay community.'

'So, you're part of a gay community, now? It's not enough to be part of the Jewish community?' Then suddenly I burst out crying. 'Oh Robert,' I sobbed. 'How could you do this to your father and me?'

'Gloria, Gloria!' Morry mumbled into his hands.

I turned on him angrily. 'Morry, our son's just told us he's a pervert. Is that all you can say – Gloria, Gloria?'

Robert bit his lip. 'I'm not a pervert, Mum,' he said, drawing himself up.

'I didn't mean it. I'm sorry. I know you're not. You're just sick. It's probably some kind of fever, picked up at those night-clubs you go to.'

At this, he sat down beside me, a half-smile playing across his lips. 'Being gay isn't a fever. It's just how I am – how I've always been.'

'Always?' I said disbelievingly.

He nodded. 'As far back as I can remember – even when I was a little child.'

'How can a little child know such a thing? How can you know for certain now? No, on second thoughts, don't tell me! But are you sure there isn't a cure?'

'I don't want one if there is, Mum,' he said. 'You see, I'm happy as I am.'

I shook my head. 'How can anyone enjoy being sick?'

'I am not sick,' he said again, this time with a touch of anger.

At this I buried my face in my hands like my husband. 'Not sick,' I repeated. 'The boy says he's not sick. If he isn't now, it won't be long before he might be. Tell me,' I added, steeling myself to broach the subject that's been hovering at the back of my mind for the last few months, 'have you thought about AIDS, Robert?'

'Of course I have, Mum. We all have. We have to. It's in the back of our minds all the time.'

'And?'

'And what?'

'Well, do you think it's sensible, turning homosexual at a time like this?'

He shrugged. 'I haven't become a homosexual by choice, Mum. As I said before, I am one, and sensible or not, that's how it is. Besides, AIDS isn't just a gay disease, you know. You must have watched all the TV programmes. It also affects heterosexuals.'

'Oh Morry, Morry,' I sobbed, oblivious to this. 'Where did we go wrong?'

For a long time we sat in silence, the three of us leaning on the table staring down at the cloth. Then at last Morry sat back, wiped the tears from his eyes and said in a croaky voice, 'I'm very sorry, son. It must be difficult for you.'

Difficult for him? What about for us? I felt like saying. But I said nothing – I just sat there as silently as the corpse I wanted at that moment to become. Because I had realized in the last few minutes that there was no point at all in my carrying on. Well, there isn't, is there, when the golden futures I'd imagined for both my children are nothing but shattered fantasies? It looks like I'm never going to be a grandmother, not if I live to be a hundred years old. And if I'm not going to be one, what do I have to look forward to? False teeth and arthritis? Wrinkles and hair loss? Another twenty-five years of cleaning the house and growing old?

Obviously this hadn't occurred to Morry. Because, 'I'm glad you told us, Robert,' he said. Then he shook his head and added, 'To tell you the truth I've suspected it for a long time. But I never said anything because I didn't want your mother to know.'

I sat bolt upright. 'What do you mean? You should have told me!'

He spread his hands. 'I'm sorry, darling, I thought I was doing the right thing.'

'Anyway,' I went on. 'Did you think I was blind? I had my suspicions, too.'

Now his brow clouded over. 'So why didn't you say anything to me?'

'I . . . I was worried that if you found out you might have a heart attack.'

'I'm his father, aren't I? And I'm a healthy man, for God's sake, not an invalid . . .'

Robert drew in his breath in a loud hiss. 'Oh, I've really set the cat among the pigeons, haven't I? Look, both of you, I'm very sorry that it's causing an argument . . .'

'Your father and I never argue. We're having a discussion.'

'And I'm sorry I never told you before.'

'Don't be, darling,' I sobbed, bursting into tears again. 'Believe me, you saved me years of heartbreak. I may have had my suspicions before, but at least I could live in hope that you might have a happy future.'

'I might still have one, Mum,' he said, putting an arm around me.

I blew my nose. 'How?' I sniffed.

'I can find happiness on my own terms. Believe me, it's not impossible. For all you know I already have.'

Then Morry and I looked at each other, and, for the first time in our thirty-six-year marriage, the same thought came simultaneously into both our heads. I know this because the next instant he said the exact words I was about to: 'You say you've been a secret homosexual for years, Robert. So why have you decided to tell us about it now?'

There was a long pause – so long I thought it'd last for ever. Then for the first time that evening, Robert's cheeks flushed a deep, embarrassed pink. 'You know this new flat I've just bought?' he said. 'Well, I'm not moving in there alone. You see, I've met someone I love – someone very special. He's called Peter. We're going to live together. And if you really love me – which I know you do – I'm sure that one day you'll learn to love him, too.'

I will, will I? Robert's got another think coming. Believe me, if I get my hands on this dirty old man who's corrupted my innocent baby, I'm going to kill him, that's what I'm going to do!

Tuesday, 28th October

First Robert. Now Sharon. If what happened on the weekend doesn't give Morry a heart attack, what Claudia told me this morning surely will. And if it doesn't give him a heart attack, I'm going to have one. I deserve to, don't I, when you consider what I'm going through.

In order to take my mind off Robert, I telephoned Claudia at work this morning to ask her a question about my book. After our lunch, I felt quite apprehensive about how she would react to a phone call at work. But, to my surprise, she sounded genuinely pleased to hear from me.

'Ah, Gloria,' she said, her gravelly voice rising on a note of gossipy delight. For the first time in years she sounded more like the Jewish girl I'd grown up with in Edgware than the Oxford graduate she pretends to be.

'Claudia, dear, I'm sorry to disturb you at work.'

'Not at all! In fact I was going to ring you up myself this morning.'

'Oh?' I said, surprised. 'What for?'

'What for? Oh, no reason in particular,' she said airily. 'Just for a friendly chat to see how you are.'

My heart swelled with real pleasure. So she did like me after all! I'd come to think that she didn't want to know me any more now that she's a publishing bigwig and I'm only an ordinary housewife. Now I saw that I'd misjudged her. 'That's nice,' I said. 'How are you, dear?'

'Marvellous, darling. And how are you?'

How was I? 'Just fine,' I lied. 'And Martin?'

'Great! And Morry?'

'Morry's fine,' I said. What else could I tell her? That he's heartbroken about Robert? The very thought of telling anyone makes me shudder.

'Good, good,' she said, rather distractedly. 'Oh, hold on a second, darling, will you? Someone's just come in. No, no, Sasha, that jacket's not really what we're looking for, is it? Sorry, darling, I'm back. Where were we?'

'I'm disturbing you, aren't I?' I apologized. 'I'll call you another time.'

'No, don't go! You know that I'm always delighted to drop what I'm doing and talk to you,' she said. Then she must have remembered our last meeting, because she suddenly added, 'Honestly I am, Gloria. Really. How's that book of yours going, by the way? Are you ready to show it to me yet?'

'Not exactly. To be frank, I've had one or two things on my mind lately.'

'Such as?' she said eagerly.

'Oh, you know, this and that. Actually, I rang because I wanted to ask your advice,' I went on, quickly changing the subject.

'Yes?'

I swallowed hard and summoned up my courage. 'How long exactly should an autobiography be?'

There was a long pause, during which I realized I knew exactly how she was going to answer: 'Well, that rather depends, doesn't it, on how much the author has to say? In the case of an ex-Prime Minister, well, a hundred to a hundred and twenty thousand words. In your case . . .' She took a deep breath. 'Remember, finding a publisher for memoirs can be jolly difficult, darling.'

I bit my lip. 'I'm sure.'

'Even though I'll bet your manuscript is fascinating. Only autobiography . . . well, it's a difficult genre to sell. Unless, as I've told you before, one's someone.'

And I'm no one, I thought miserably, no one at all – not even the good housewife and mother I've always tried to be.

'Gloria?' she said, noting my silence. 'I haven't offended you, have I?'

'No! Of course not. Why should you?' I said, giving a false laugh.

'Oh good, darling. Because I'm simply dying to read your manuscript, really I am.'

'Thank you,' I said flatly. To tell the truth, nothing scares me more than the thought of showing my manuscript (or what there is of it) to Claudia. Or, rather let me say that at that particular moment, in my blissful ignorance of what she was about to tell me, nothing could have scared me more.

'I'm sorry to have wasted your time,' I grovelled.

'Darling, you haven't wasted my time at all,' she said warmly. 'It's always a pleasure to talk to you. You know, we haven't talked enough lately. In fact, I've been a little concerned about you, to tell you the truth.'

'Whatever for?'

'I don't know. Call me a silly-billy if you like, but ever since we had lunch together I've had this vague sort of feeling there's something troubling you, something on your mind.'

'Such as?' I asked suspiciously.

'Oh, I don't know. It's probably nothing but my silly imagination running away with me.' She cleared her throat. 'How *are* the children, by the way?'

I froze. Could she have heard about Robert so quickly? I mean, I know news travels fast around our way, but I certainly hadn't expected it to reach Hampstead in three days. I myself haven't told a soul since I learned about it, not even Ruth or Angel. 'Robert's fine,' I said firmly.

'Of course.' Her tone was dismissive. 'And Sharon?'

'She's fine, too.'

'Ah,' she said, and fell into a thoughtful silence.

'Why do you ask?' I asked.

'Oh, no particular reason. I just wondered if . . .' She stopped.

'If?' I prompted.

'Nothing. Nothing. I was being silly. I don't think I expected you to be so broad-minded, that's all.'

My blood froze. 'Oh?' I said. 'How do you mean?'

'Oh, you know.' I grunted. Frankly I did not know, but I wasn't going to give her the satisfaction of not knowing something about my own child that she did. 'I

III

bumped into her yesterday, actually, at lunch, upstairs at L'Escargot,' she went on with studied casualness. 'And, do you know, she was looking quite, quite divine.'

'Really?' I said, now genuinely surprised.

'Radiant, one might say.' Again Claudia hesitated. 'Funny, you never told me she was seeing someone,' she went on at last.

'You never asked,' I said quickly. Then my stomach turned to stone.

'They seemed very fond of each other.' Here she giggled. 'And they make a jolly handsome couple, don't they? He's, um, awfully good-looking, isn't he?' she went on carefully.

'Oh, do you think so?'

'Mmm. So tall and . . . and exotic. He looks just like Lenny Henry, doesn't he?'

'Well,' I waffled, trying to remember where I'd heard the name before. 'Perhaps a little. Just around the eyes. Just around the . . .'

Suddenly I remembered that I'd heard the name Lenny Henry on television.

Oh yes, Lenny Henry is a comic.

Oh, yes, I've even seen his show.

And, oh yes, suddenly my heart stopped beating. Frankly, wouldn't any mother's heart have? I mean, I realized what Claudia was getting at.

No wonder she thinks I'm broad-minded.

Lenny Henry is black.

I'm not a racist. Of course I'm not. How could I be when I am Jewish? We who have suffered persecution ourselves know better than to judge others by the colour of their skin. One must, and one does, take a stand about these things. Believe me, if Claudia is right when she says my daughter is going out with a *shvartzer*, you can take it on trust that I don't object to him because he's a black man, only because he's an unsuitable boyfriend for my Sharon. She picked him, didn't she, so he's bound to be.

I have just closed my eyes, and tried to imagine the scene in the synagogue when they get married, but the image won't come. No wonder: if he's black, there'll be no synagogue because he won't be Jewish, unless of course he's a Falasha. And if by some remote chance he is, Sharon won't marry him anyway, not if he begged her. Because my Sharon doesn't believe in marriage, just as she doesn't believe in fur coats, nuclear power, cosmetic surgery, maternal urges or cutting her hair.

Dear God, tell me something, will you? How did I, Gloria Gold of Anson Avenue, Hendon, have two such children? Were they changelings, or did I go wrong somewhere? I certainly didn't bring them up to behave like this. And yet they must have learned this behaviour from someone. It's enough to make you sit down and cry.

I am crying now. My mascara has dripped all over the keyboard. I think I'll write a little note to remind myself to buy a waterproof one to wear in future. It looks like I'm going to need it during the next few weeks.

Dear God, give me guidance, I beg You. Tell me what I ought to do with this daughter of mine. Do I just sit back and let her ruin her life like Robert's ruined his, or do I do something about it?

Wait a minute! Am I not jumping the gun, rather? Am I not presupposing that what Claudia told me is true? Might it be that my dear friend – who is blind as a bat without her spectacles, but often doesn't wear them for vanity's sake – that she might have been wrong in thinking she saw Sharon and this black man canoodling together in a restaurant? Might it not be that Claudia, in her old age – which, however much she lies about it, is exactly the same as mine – has gone a little colour-blind? That would explain a lot, wouldn't it? Even her liking for those dun-coloured Japanese designer clothes. And if she is colour-blind *and* short-sighted, there's a good chance she was mistaken! I suddenly feel better! Oh, what a relief! I always knew that, though wild at times, Sharon was basically sensible. And any basically sensible person would know that a black man is not an appropriate boyfriend for a nice Jewish girl.

They would, wouldn't they? It's only right, isn't it? Any mother, black or white, would agree with me?

But what if Claudia isn't colour-blind and Sharon really is going out with a black man? Worse – what if this black man is the 'flatmate' I'm not allowed to meet? He doesn't sound black on the phone but . . . Oh no, I can't bear the thought of it! There's only one thing for it – I'll have to go and see.

Saturday, 1st November

I shouldn't have done what I did, but I did it, so what can I do about it now? Was it so terrible? To drop in unexpectedly on Sharon at five-past eight this morning, in that flat in Kentish Town? Why did I not do it years ago? If I'd only been a bit more resourceful when she was younger, this tragedy might never have happened. As it was, I have let her get away with far too much for far too long. Now it's probably too late to do anything about it. That girl has ruined my life.

Finding out where she lived turned out to be surprisingly easy. When I think of all the hours I've wasted in the past pleading with her for the address! And in the end all it took was one phone-call to the personnel department of that television company she works for. Oh yes, and a few carefully rehearsed lies.

'Hallo,' I said into the receiver. 'Please can I speak to the man in charge?'

'I am in charge,' said a woman's voice. 'Can I ask who's speaking, please?'

'My name's Mrs Gold. I'm Sharon's mother.'

'Sharon Gold? Oh yes, of course I know Sharon. Well, nice to speak to you, Mrs Gold. What can I do for you?'

I took a deep breath and jumped in at the deep end. 'I was wondering if you could tell me where Sharon's living at the moment?'

'Don't you know?' she asked in a surprised voice.

'No, as a matter of fact I don't.'

'Oh, I see,' she said. And added suspiciously, 'Um . . . isn't that a bit unusual?'

'I suppose it must seem so to you,' I said. 'But you see, I've been out of the country for some months, and I've only just come back. And I know Sharon was thinking of moving, so I'm ringing you to find out if she has.'

'Oh, I see. Um, wouldn't she have written to tell you if she was moving?'

Here I realized that the woman was going to be difficult, and I was going to be forced to tell more than a single lie. 'I was on safari,' I said. 'There wasn't much opportunity for receiving letters.'

'Oh?'

'Of course, she was going to let me know where she was when I came back, but you see, she didn't expect me for another two months. I came home early, after contracting a touch of malaria.'

'Oh dear, I'm sorry to hear it. You must be feeling terrible.'

'Yes, I am,' I answered truthfully.

There was a long pause. 'Look, I'm sorry if I seem difficult, Mrs Gold,' she said. 'But for security reasons we have a policy in this company not to give out our employees' addresses over the telephone.'

Had Sharon already warned this woman about me? I wondered suddenly. 'I'm not a security risk,' I said with a touch of anger. 'I'm her mother.'

'I'm sure you are. You know you are. But to me, you see, you're just a voice on the end of the telephone. And I'm sure you'd be the first to appreciate my caution. So before I give you her address, I must satisfy myself that —'

'Of course, of course.'

'Well, couldn't you call her old telephone number and see if she's still living there?' she suggested.

Now what was I going to say? 'No, I couldn't.'

'May I ask you why not?'

'Because . . . Because I can never remember telephone numbers,' I said on the spur of the moment. 'I don't have that sort of brain.'

'Well, don't you have an address book?'

'Not any more,' I lied, almost without thinking. 'It fell into the river in Africa, and before I could fish it out it was snapped up by a crocodile. I nearly lost three fingers trying to save it.'

There was a gasp at the other end of the line. 'Gosh,' the woman said. 'Sharon never mentioned she had such an adventurous mother!' And after that she gave me the address with no trouble at all.

The next thing I had to do was to get away from the house at 7.30 this morning without letting Morry know where I was going. I had imagined that deceiving him would be difficult, but it turned out to be quite the opposite.

'Morry,' I said last night, when we were sitting side by side on the sofa watching television. 'I forgot to tell you something.' He looked up from the thriller he was reading, not at me but at the TV screen, and he turned over a page of his book absent-mindedly. Though his habit of reading while he watches television usually drives me to distraction, I was more than grateful for his pre-occupation for once. 'My synagogue committee is holding a charity bazaar on Monday,' I said casually.

'Very nice, dear.'

'We've rented a hall in Edgware.'

'Marvellous,' he murmured, lowering the book and changing TV channels with the remote controls.

My hackles rose, despite myself. 'I was watching that!' I said in a hurt voice.

'Sorry, darling. Didn't realize.' Without looking up from his book again, he switched back to the original channel.

'Thank you,' I muttered. 'Anyway, the committee couldn't get access to the hall until tomorrow, Morry. So we're going to have to get everything ready for the bazaar then.'

'I see.' He looked up at me with a frown on his innocent forehead. 'But tomorrow's Saturday, isn't it?' he said. 'I thought some of those women were religious. Surely they won't work on the Sabbath?'

I shrugged. 'God won't mind – it's to raise money for Kosher Meals-on-Wheels. I'm going to have to be there very early in the morning, Morry. I should be back by lunchtime.'

'Don't overdo it, Gloria,' he said. 'Don't work too hard.'

Sharon was furious when she saw me standing on the doorstep of the small terraced house she lives in – but furious more with embarrassment than with anything else. When she opened the front door, she gasped in horror. 'What are you doing here?' she said, clasping a skimpy cotton dressing-gown around her.

'I couldn't sleep with worrying about your brother, so I got up early and did the laundry you brought home the other day. Anyway, since you were too busy to come for dinner last night, I thought it'd save you time if I dropped it in myself, rather than you having to come over and collect it. Then perhaps you'll have a little more time to devote to a social life this evening.'

Her pale skin coloured. 'Thank you,' she said in a voice that was anything but grateful. One hand shot out and took the laundry-bag from me, the other held firmly on to the door.

'It's a pleasure,' I said, smiling as nicely as I could. There was an awkward pause. Then,

'Well, I've got to go,' she said, starting to shut the door. 'I'm afraid I'm rather busy. I've got to be at work soon.'

'On a Saturday?' I said as I planted my foot firmly over the threshold. 'No one works on a Saturday. And you know, the drive from Hendon has left me rather thirsty. After all the meals I've made you over the years, do you mind if I trouble you for a single cup of tea?'

She turned pale, and bit her lip, and glanced over her shoulder, and in that moment, I suddenly realized that what Claudia had told me might be true. There was a man in that flat, and she didn't want me to meet him. 'You won't like my tea,' she said quickly. 'I've only got herbal.'

'I'll have a glass of water if I don't like it,' I said. I waited for her to move away from the door, but she remained there like a guard dog. 'So are you going to leave me here all day, standing on your doorstep like a common pedlar?' I said after a time. 'I'm getting cold out here, darling. And you'll catch pneumonia in that thin thing you're wearing. And did you know you've left your dustbin just outside the gate? Don't you think you should put it away?'

When I said this, I knew I'd put my foot in it somehow and lost the advantage, because the shock of seeing me began to drain away from her face, and in its place appeared that oh-so-familiar anger. 'I have put it away,' she said in the clipped tone she reserves for talking to me. 'That's where it belongs.'

'What, out in the street?' I exclaimed.

'Yes, out in the street. Along with all the others.'

I glanced down the road and saw a long line of bins stretching into the distance. 'That's the most unhealthy thing I've ever seen! Why don't your neighbours use their dustbin sheds?'

'Because they don't have any.'

'Well then, they ought to build some!'

'Look, Mum, this isn't Hendon. People round here don't have money to throw around.'

'Darling,' I laughed. 'You don't have to be a millionaire to buy a few planks of wood and some nails and a hammer.'

Just then, a small tortoiseshell cat scampered down the hall and proceeded to rub its pointed head ingratiatingly against Sharon's bare feet. 'Hallo Gremlin,' she said, picking it up and hoisting it over her shoulder where it drooped like a cheap fur collar, purring loudly and glaring defiantly at me.

'Sharon!' I said in a shocked voice. 'Not so near your face! You don't know where it's been!'

By now, Sharon's eyes were blazing as angrily as the

cat's. 'How did you find out where I lived?' she snapped.
I shrugged. 'Did Robert tell you?'

'I never knew he knew the address.'

She made a face. 'Of course he knows. He's my brother.
Then who? Someone must have told you.'

'Actually I found out for myself. Remember, you inherited your brains from someone. Now,' I added, trying
to peer past her down the hall, 'how about that cup of
tea you promised me?'

She put the cat down. 'Look, it's a bit early. The place
is in an awful mess. Why don't you come round later this
afternoon – for tea or something – when I've had a chance
to tidy up?'

'Oh, a little bit of mess won't bother me!' I exclaimed.
She looked sceptical.

Suddenly a sleepy man's voice spoke from the back of
the hall: 'Who's there, darling?' My heart stopped. I have
a feeling that Sharon's did too, because she turned even
paler than she already was, and glanced inside.

'It's all right, thank you, Benedict,' she said, her voice
loaded with meaning. 'It's only my mother.'

Only your mother, I thought, after bringing you into
the world at the expense of my figure? Only your mother,
after all the years I've sacrificed myself for you? As she
tried to pull the door closer, I wedged my foot more
firmly under it, took hold of the arm that was barring my
way and tried to force it down.

'That must be this flatmate I've heard so much about,'
I said. 'Aren't you going to introduce me to him?'

'Let go of me, Mum!'

For a few seconds we grappled on the doorstep. Then
she sighed with resignation and her arms fell limply to
her sides. 'Oh, for God's sake,' she said. 'This is demean-
ing. Look, since you're here, you might as well come in

and see for yourself. I suppose you've been speaking to Claudia, haven't you?'

I felt sick. 'Claudia?' I laughed with false brightness. 'Whatever makes you say that?'

She stepped aside and threw the door open. Suddenly I was overcome with a strange fit of nerves. For what would I find inside this flat I had waited five long years to see? Brushing past her, I walked into a bare, narrow, carpeted hall.

'Quite nice,' I muttered, glancing around me. Then I stopped dead in my tracks. 'What's a bicycle doing in here?'

'It's Benedict's.'

'I don't care whose it is,' I said, squeezing past it. 'What's it doing in the hall? Why isn't it outside in the street where it belongs?'

'Because it'd get stolen.'

I looked at her colourless cheeks with concern. 'He shouldn't bring it inside. Think of the dirt on the wheels! No wonder you look so peaky. Really, Sharon, it's not hygienic —'

'Mum!'

Shut up, I told myself, because if you're not careful she'll throw you out before you've seen anything. 'And what's in here?' I said, starting to push open a door.

'That's my bedroom,' she said, and grabbing hold of the handle she quickly pulled it shut. 'Don't bother going in there,' she said. 'It's a terrible mess. I haven't made the bed yet.'

I raised my eyebrows. 'Really, dear, I won't be shocked. I've seen an unmade bed before.'

'I'm sure you have,' she said, steering me firmly onwards towards the sound of clinking crockery that was coming from the end of the hall. 'Look, come into the kitchen.

I'm sure you'd like to meet Benedict, wouldn't you?' she added in a voice laden with sarcasm.

The door swung open, and at first all I could see was a windowful of potted plants and a bare kitchen table still damp from being wiped clean. Then I heard a cupboard close, and a muscular giant in a T-shirt and jeans unfurled from a squatting position behind the table with a J-cloth in his hand. I caught my breath: Claudia had been wrong – he looked more like a young Sidney Poitier than like Lenny Henry. When he saw me standing there he smiled broadly and put the J-cloth on the table. Then he wiped his hands on his jeans and came towards me with one outstretched in greeting.

'You must be Sharon's mother,' he said in one of the poshest English accents I have ever heard. 'Sharon's told me so much about you. Great to meet you at last.'

Truthfully, that's all I can remember of this morning. What happened afterwards is just a great big blank. Sharon made coffee, and we sat around the table making awkward small-talk. Of the three of us, only Benedict seemed at all at ease. He chatted freely about his job as a television drama producer and his school-days (it turns out he was at Eton), and when I asked him where he came from (a remark that provoked Sharon into exclaiming 'Mother!' in a particularly deprecating way) he told me that his family had come over here from Nigeria in the late 1950s as political refugees, and that his father had been the chief of a tribe. When I asked him if he would be chief too one day, he laughed and said, no, the title would pass to one of his older brothers, and anyway he wasn't chief material, he was only an ordinary prince.

The final blow that broke my heart in pieces descended on me just as I was leaving. As I stood on the doorstep, I asked the question I now know I should never have asked: as far as I could tell, I said, Sharon had shown me all the flat – so where was the second bedroom? At this the two of them smiled at each other. Then Sharon blushed and said, 'Mum, haven't you realized?' 'Realized what?' I said desperately. She looked at Benedict again and shrugged. 'I guess she's got to know some time,' she muttered. Then she slipped her arm around his waist and looked at me with a hopeful smile. 'Mum, darling,' she said gently. 'Benedict shares a room with me.'

About an hour ago I staggered home, and told Morry what I had discovered. When the initial shock wore off, he phoned up Sharon and invited himself over for a cup of herbal tea. I only hope he sorts the matter out once and for all, as he said he would. Otherwise, I don't see what future is left for me.

It is 4.30 and Morry just arrived back from Sharon's flat. He came into the kitchen with a strange, closed expression on his face.

'Well? What happened?' I said, putting a cup of coffee and a large chopped-liver-on-rye sandwich in front of him as he sat down at the kitchen table.

'Give me a minute,' he said, stretching out his legs and pushing the sandwich away. 'I'm not very hungry, thank you, Gloria.'

'I'm not surprised,' I said. 'That girl has taken away your appetite.'

'Actually, I had lunch there.'

I looked at him in horror. 'Lunch? Do you mean you sat down and ate at that filthy kitchen table?'

'It looked clean enough to me.'

'To you, maybe.' I shook my head. 'Well, I only hope you didn't pick up a stomach bug,' I added as I put away the loaf of bread.

Morry frowned. 'Don't exaggerate. The girl is perfectly healthy. In fact, they both are.'

What's this 'both'? I thought. 'What did she give you, brown rice and nuts?'

'Actually, we had bacon and spinach salad.'

My mouth dropped open. 'Morry, bacon on a Saturday!'

'So what? Do you think God doesn't know I eat bacon during the rest of the week?'

'Not in my house you don't,' I sniffed as I pulled on a pair of rubber gloves and wiped the draining board with a square of kitchen towel. 'Well, did she grill the bacon or fry it?' I asked. 'Did you check that her grill pan was clean?'

'No, Gloria, I did not check,' he said with straining patience. 'And as a matter of fact, she didn't cook anything. Benedict did. And I might tell you, it was delicious.'

Grabbing hold of a Brillo pad, I began to scour the sink. 'Oh, I see,' I said. 'Well, did you sort the matter out?' I went on nervously.

'What matter?'

I rubbed furiously at a stain in the left-hand corner. 'You-know-what matter, Morry. The matter you went round to discuss.'

'Ah, that,' he said vaguely. 'Oh . . . well . . .'

'Well, what?'

'Well, there isn't much to sort out.'

I laughed. 'You and your jokes!' I said. Which fell rather flat, because frankly Morry hasn't made half a dozen jokes since I married him. 'No, seriously,' I added.

'I am being serious, Gloria,' he said, scraping his chair back and standing up. 'What can one do? Sharon's a grown-up woman. And though Benedict's not the man I would have chosen for her, I have to admit he's a very nice lad.'

I dropped the Brillo, pulled off my rubber gloves, and rounded on him in amazement. 'But he's black,' I said.

Morry shrugged. 'Do you think I didn't notice? Naturally he's black. He's a Nigerian.'

'Well then!'

'Well then what?'

'Well then, he's not suitable, is he?'

Morry took a deep breath. 'I don't see why not. Oh, Gloria, don't look at me like that! We're Jews. We know what it's like to be discriminated against. Talking to them made me realize that we can't disapprove of Benedict because of his colour. It would be like turning our backs on all who died in the Holocaust. What were all those millions of deaths for, if not to teach us a thing or two about racial prejudice? Benedict may be black but he's a nice boy from a good family. Why, he told me he's even some sort of prince-in-exile.'

'Mazeltov!' I said, bursting into tears. 'Let's go out and celebrate. Our Jewish princess has found a prince! Let's hire the King David Suite. Let's invite the whole family. Let's put an announcement in the *Jewish Chronicle*. "Morris and Gloria Gold announce a double wedding – Sharon and her *shvartzer*, Robert and his . . . his *friend*!"'

Morris's face fell suddenly. 'Don't be like that,' he said. 'Things may not have turned out as we wanted them for our children, but we've got to let them find their own happiness. We've got to let them lead their own lives. They're no longer little kids. They're old enough to make their own decisions.'

'Don't give me all that, Morry!' I cried. 'You sound like you've been talking to Sharon.'

'Darling, that's what I went round there for.'

Sunday, 2nd November

The joys of motherhood? Who would be a mother nowadays? For anyone who's thinking of starting on this particular venture, let me give you a small word of advice: don't. Believe me, the business of motherhood is not as easy as you may have been led to expect.

What do we know of it before we have a baby? Does anyone tell us how hard and heartbreaking it's going to be? Oh no! They tell us it's all marvellous and natural and easy. But easy it isn't.

First there's the pain of giving birth. Then there's the fear when the nurses hand the screaming bundle back to you and shove you out of the maternity ward. After that, you're on your own for all the sleepless nights and worried days, and however you do or don't bring them up, there's always some theorist or other to disapprove. Spock, schmock, it doesn't matter whose advice you take. Because after all the years of blood and tears, just at the point when you've grown experienced enough to think that you've brought them up right, your kids will turn around and kick you in the teeth just to let you know you've done everything wrong.

When I was a child, things were different. Parents in those days used to be able to expect things from their children. But now everything is different. And how! Today, youngsters have no respect for their elders. Far from it: they expect you to have respect for them. Not only that, they expect you to love and cherish them unconditionally, without ever questioning their motives, no matter what awful things they do or say. And there's worse: whatever they decide to do in the ignorance of their meagre years, you not only have to help them do it, you have to approve of it, too. Though your heart may be breaking as you watch them throw away their chances of marriage or become a homosexual or sniff glue, it's not enough for you to smile and say, Mazeltov! You have to actually *think* it! Because if you accidentally let slip that you might not like what they're doing, that's an unforgivable crime, that's being a bigot, a racist, a bad mother. And don't think that you can count on your husband to support you if you criticize your children. Just remember this – no one has respect for a housewife's views.

Don't let anyone fool you about the joys of motherhood. In my experience they just don't exist.

5

Maturity and Me

It is 10.00 a.m. and I have just forced myself to get out of bed, where I have been lying since late yesterday afternoon. I just couldn't rouse myself last night, not even to make Morry a salt-beef sandwich for supper.

'Make it yourself,' I called from the pillows when he shouted up from downstairs that he wanted one.

'How?' he said.

'Take two bits of bread, hold them half-an-inch apart and put a couple of slices of beef in between.'

'What about the mustard?' he yelled.

'What about it?' I yelled back.

'What should I do with it?'

'Do what you like with it, Morry,' I croaked. 'For all I care you can smear it on your head.'

There was a long pause. Then I heard his footsteps plod slowly and gravely upstairs, and his frowning face peered round the door. 'What's the matter with you tonight?' he said in a curious voice.

I smiled grimly. 'What should be the matter with me? I've never felt better in my life.'

He came across and sat down on the edge of the bed.

'Gloria,' he sighed. 'I know it's a bad time, but believe me, things will improve.'

'Sure they will,' I smiled. 'Robert will get AIDS, Sharon will emigrate to Africa, Angel Dresses will go bankrupt because Ruth hasn't any mid-season samples to sell. Soon there'll be nothing left to worry about.'

He took my hand. 'This isn't like you,' he said. 'Sounding so bitter.'

I laughed. 'What do I have to be bitter about?' I lay back on the pillows and half-closed my eyes. 'I'm sure things like these happen to most people once in a while.'

He sighed again, and, standing up, went over to the door. 'One or two?' he asked suddenly, turning towards me.

'What are you talking about?'

'Do you want one or two sandwiches?'

I shuddered. 'Do you think I've got an appetite? Maybe you, Morry, have no feelings and can eat at a time like this, but I certainly can't. Well, perhaps I could force down a small one,' I called after him as he went out of the door. But not this small, I thought to myself forty-five minutes later when, after there'd been so much crashing and bashing about downstairs I'd thought that the Third World War had broken out in my broom cupboard, he brought up a few crumbs on a dinner plate. My curiosity whetted, I put on a dressing-gown and crawled down to the kitchen. What had he been doing in there all this time?

I opened the door, and saw, with grim satisfaction, for myself. I was on the point of shouting at Morry when the telephone rang, and Ruth was on the line.

'Gloria, you haven't rung me for days,' she complained.

'I know.'

'Why not? Is this any time to ignore your sister?'

'I'm sorry,' I croaked. 'I've had one or two things on my mind.' I took a deep breath. 'Robert . . .' I began.

'Yes, I know, darling,' she said, her voice suddenly sympathetic. 'And I'm very, very sorry. But why didn't you tell me?'

'I don't know – I didn't want to trouble you with things as they are. Any news from –?'

'No,' she interrupted me. 'Not a word. I don't understand, Gloria. I thought if I let him have a long rein he'd be back in five minutes. But it doesn't look like it. And things at the business are terrible. I don't know how I'll manage without those samples. Oh Christ, where did I go wrong?'

'Where did I go wrong?' I echoed.

We both sighed, and tut-tutted for a moment in wordless commiseration. 'How did you find out about Robert?' I asked eventually.

'He rang me at work this morning and told me, and asked me whether or not I thought he should tell Angel.'

'Oh my God! What does he want to tell people for? The less said to anyone about this the better.'

'You can hardly keep it a secret, Gloria,' Ruth said. 'Isn't telling people the whole point of his coming out?'

'He can go straight back in, as far as I'm concerned,' I said firmly. 'And as for telling Mummy – I absolutely forbid it!'

'You're a bit late, Gloria,' she said gently. 'She already knows.'

My fingers tightened around the receiver. 'What?' I gasped.

'She happened to be here when he called, and she grabbed the phone from me before I could stop her.'

I sank down on the telephone seat and stared blankly

at the directories. 'Oh no! Poor Mummy, she must have been broken-hearted!'

'Not exactly,' Ruth said slowly. 'Funnily enough, it seems that she's known for years.'

'How could she have known? Tell me, what did she say?'

'One of the things she said was, "How could Gloria not have known all these years? Is my daughter blind?" But her very first words were, "So you've found the courage to admit it at last! Well, Robert, now I'm proud to call you my grandson."'

I shook my head. So his grandmother was proud of him? Was Angel completely mad? And then it occurred to me that she might well be mad, and if so it was probably from her that Robert and Sharon have inherited their peculiarities. ⊁

'And then she said, "Well, I only hope you know what you're doing, Robert, and that you're having safe sex."'

'What?' I said, sitting bolt upright.

'You heard me, Gloria. That's what she said.'

'What's Mummy afraid of?' I muttered sarcastically. 'That Robert will get pregnant?'

'Well, I could hear Robert laughing down the telephone, and he shrieked, "Grandma, you're incredible!"'

'That's one word for her. Honestly, how does Mummy even know about things like safe sex?'

'Apparently she's watched all the AIDS programmes on TV. I said to her, wasn't it a bit personal talking to Robert about such things and she said, "For God's sake, Ruth, must you pretend that sex doesn't exist?"'

'It makes a change for Mummy to say that to you,' I said. 'Usually Sharon's saying it to me.' I paused for a moment and let out a long sigh. 'What a life!'

'Isn't it just, Gloria? It's a good thing we've got each

other to rely on, isn't it? What with Mark and that bitch, and Robert – and Sharon.'

I groaned. 'So you know about her, too? News travels fast. Did Robert tell you yesterday?'

'Oh no, Sharon rang me up and told me you'd been round, just after you'd gone home. It must have been quite a shock for you.'

'What do you think? To tell the truth, I thought I was going to have a heart attack.'

'Poor Gloria, what a way to find out. Honestly, I told her ages ago she ought to tell you because if she didn't you'd only find out for yourself some day.'

'Well, it certainly was a –' I stopped. My ears buzzed. 'What did you just say?'

'I said I told her ages ago to . . .' Her voice trailed off into an uneasy silence. Then she drew in her breath in a most unladylike whistle. 'Oh Lord! Look, darling, let me explain.'

'What is there to explain?' I said coldly. 'You knew about it, did you?'

'Look, Gloria, I –'

'You knew! For how long?'

'I don't know. Nine months. Maybe a year.'

A year. I felt as breathless as if she had kicked me in the stomach. 'You knew for a whole year that my daughter was seeing that man, and you didn't tell me?'

'I couldn't,' she said lamely. 'Sharon told me in confidence.'

'But I'm your sister!'

'Yes, I know, Gloria. But Sharon's my niece. And she's an adult now. And I had to respect her wishes – just as, if I told you something in confidence, I'd expect you to respect mine.'

'But Ruth, I'm the girl's mother. I only have her best

interests at heart. Why, if you even suspected she was doing something wrong behind my back, you had a duty to tell me! Just as, if I'd suspected about Mark and Hattie, I'd have had a duty to tell you.' Under the circumstances, this was not the best analogy I could have made. Because I had suspected that very thing, hadn't I, and I hadn't said a word.

'That's different,' Ruth said defensively. 'What Mark and Hattie were doing was wrong. Whereas, what Sharon is doing is living her own life.'

'Ruining it, you mean. And you, her aunt, were prepared to stand by and let her do that?'

'As a matter of fact, I don't think she is ruining her life, Gloria. After all, she's only living with the man she loves. What's wrong about that? I know these things take a little adjusting to, I know it's unusual that he's Nigerian, to say the least but . . . I don't expect you to like what I'm going to say, but I'm going to say it anyway: I've got to know Benedict quite well over the last few months, and he's an extremely nice man.'

'Whether he's nice or not is immaterial. The point is that he's black.'

'Don't be so prejudiced.'

'I'm not prejudiced!'

'Yes you are!'

'No, I'm not. I'm just being practical. Everyone knows that mixed marriages don't work. Though I know Sharon doesn't think so at the moment, she'd be much better off with a Jewish husband, someone who understands her culture and her religion.'

Here Ruth sighed. 'Gloria,' she said. 'You're making out that daughter of yours is some kind of rabbi. When the truth is that she's no more religious than you or I.'

What was she getting at? 'How dare you!' I said. 'Why,

I always light candles on Friday nights, don't I? And I keep a fairly Kosher home.'

'You told me yourself that the only reason you don't eat bacon is that you're convinced it'll give you tape-worms. Besides, that's not what I meant by being religious. When was the last time you went to a synagogue?'

'Yom Kippur, naturally.'

'Everyone goes on Yom Kippur, Gloria. That doesn't mean a thing. But do you believe in it all? Do you really believe?'

What was this – the Inquisition? And what had this got to do with Sharon and that man? By now, I was dangerously close to losing my restrained temper. 'Yes, as a matter of fact I do believe, Ruth – I believe you ought to mind your own business.'

'I have minded my own business, Gloria. That's why I never said anything to you when Sharon told me about Benedict. I felt it wasn't my business to interfere.'

'Really! It's all right for you to be so bloody liberal when your own daughter is married to a Hassid and lives in Jerusalem and has three children.'

'That's not fair, Gloria!' she protested. 'Believe me, I'd much rather she was working in television and living here! I wish – yes, I'd give anything for a daughter like Sharon!'

First Claudia and now Ruth, I thought. What is it with my Sharon? Everyone thinks she's the perfect daughter – everyone, that is, except me. I don't understand it, I really don't. Why, they should try being her mother. Five minutes, I'd give them – that's four-and-a-half minutes too long for me.

By now Ruth had dissolved into tears, and I was beginning to feel like I used to when we were in the day nursery with Nanny – as if I'd made her cry. 'Who have

I got to turn to when things go wrong?' she sobbed. 'It's all right for you, you've got Morry. I've got no one any more – no one at all.'

'You've got me,' I said grudgingly. And added, 'I'm a loyal sister.'

'Oh darling, I'm sorry I didn't tell you! But Sharon did tell me in confidence. What was I supposed to do?'

Break the bloody confidence, I should have said. I mean, if Sharon had told her that she was a drug addict, would she have kept silent about that too? However, by that time Ruth sounded so upset that I bit my tongue and said nothing. Instead, after putting down the receiver I trudged up to bed and took some Valium, and forgot all about scolding Morry about the state of the kitchen.

As I write this down, I'm beginning to feel terribly angry with Ruth again, and to wonder why I made up with her. When I think of all the times I've confided my worries about Sharon to her, and all the time she knew exactly what was going on! She was probably laughing at me behind my back. Why, I could kill her, I really could. I'd like to take her by the throat right now and shake her till her bones rattled . . .

I'm getting carried away. Of course I don't want to kill her. She's my sister, and I love her dearly. I even feel sorry for her. I mean, God knows she's got enough troubles of her own, and God forbid such a terrible thing should ever happen to me as has happened to her in the past few weeks! But still . . . Why am I feeling so uncharitable towards her at this moment? I know that being abandoned by Mark is not something that she's done on purpose, but . . . For some stupid reason I can't help feeling a little jealous of her. She's always managed to be the self-righteous one, and the centre of attention, ever since we were little girls. Whereas when have I ever been in the right? When have I been the centre of attention? It's always been, 'Pull yourself together, Gloria!' but 'Poor little Ruth!' And if it's not Ruth that people are being sympathetic towards, it's some other member of the family – 'Poor Troubled Robert!' or 'Poor Misunderstood Sharon!' or 'Poor Morry-who-can't-put-his-feet-on-the-coffee-table!' No one ever says, 'Poor Gloria!' I might as well not exist, for all the concern my family shows me. I might as well walk out of my front door right now and never come back.

And why not? None of them would miss me. They'd probably all breathe a sigh of relief if they saw me packing my bags, mutter 'Thank God!' under their breath, and 'At last we can relax!' I'd bet that Morry, who once couldn't leave me alone at night, wouldn't even notice if I wasn't sleeping next to him in our bed. If I decided to leave him, he'd probably drop me at the station with as much sorrow as if I was on my way to Brent Cross, then come home and throw the druggets and dust covers straight in the bin.

What has it all been for? I ask myself. Why, I have spent the best part of my life cooking for them, and scrubbing and cleaning and tidying this house, and to what purpose? Only to have to do it again the next day, and the day after, and the day after that. Thirty-six years of marriage. Thirty-six years of three hundred and sixty-five cleaning days. How much detergent have I flushed down the drains in that time? How many scouring pads, mops and J-Cloths have I worn through? How many containers of Persil and Daz, Domestos and Mansion Polish, Fairy and Pledge, Flash and Ajax, Silvo and Brillo, Oven-Kleen and Windolene have I used up and thrown away? Poured together they would form a vast ocean of germ-fighting, sterile, whiter-than-white suds. And where has all my hard work got me?

When I think about it, my entire existence can be summed up in six words – 'I Came, I Saw, I Cleaned'. It would have made a fitting title for an autobiography, if I had managed to write one. Instead, they can chisel it on my tombstone when I've passed away.

Hold on a minute – why am I thinking about my tombstone? Is this a premonition that I'm going to die? In a funny way, I feel that part of me is dying – the old Gloria Gold, the one who used to be so happy and contented being a housewife and mother. I only hope someone new will be born in her place.

It's nearly eleven o'clock now, and I'm still in my nightie. I suppose I'd better get dressed and go downstairs. I can't sit idling up here all day.

Oh God, I wish there was someone I could talk to about all the things that are troubling me, someone who would understand my point of view without feeling the need to give me a lecture about motherhood or equality or children's rights.

I wonder if Christian would understand? Good God, what am I saying? Confide in a man, who's neither Jewish nor my husband? I couldn't possibly!

Thursday, 6th November

I could tell Christian. I did. I know I wasn't going to, but when I walked down the corridor last night and saw him leaning against the classroom door, so tall and solid in his old tweed jacket, and when he ambled towards me with such a pleased-to-see-me smile on his face and said, 'Gloria! Where were you last week? Have you been all right?' all my resistance gave way and before I could stop myself I blurted out, 'Not really.'

His forehead furrowed. 'Have you been ill?'

Unable to say another word, I stared hard at the floor to try and stop my tears from falling. He reached over and took one of my clenched fists in his enormous warm palm, and gave it a friendly squeeze. And just when he was about to say something else, Melanie Thatcher turned into the corridor and he dropped my hand and said, 'Look, we can't talk now. Let's go out for a drink later on.'

How slowly the class passed last night, when usually the time flashes by and I'm home before I know it! I couldn't concentrate on anything that was said, I really couldn't, especially with the fireworks crashing and bashing outside as loud as the Blitz (I had quite forgotten it was Guy Fawkes Night). It seemed an eternity before the class ended and it was time to go.

'Coming to the pub, Chris?' Irene said, applying another coat of pink lipstick to her mouth.

'I'm afraid I can't tonight,' he said. 'I've got to get home.'

So his wife must have come back to him during the last fortnight. Well, good things do happen, I reflected, if not to me. Obviously, he'd forgotten about having a talk to me.

'How boring of you, Chris!' Irene giggled as she and Melanie went out the door arm in arm. 'Come on, Gerrard, coming for a pint? Dr Seal? Mrs Gold? Mrs B? Oh, don't be spoilsports, all of you!'

The room emptied. People from other classes walked past outside with echoing footsteps, and then the corridor grew silent. I was left sitting at my desk with the same heavy, despairing feeling in my tummy that's been there all week, dreading the thought of going home. Eventually I stood up and put on my coat. 'Goodbye, see you next week,' I muttered, grabbing my handbag and heading for the door.

He frowned. 'Where are you going? Aren't we having our drink?'

'But you just said . . .' I began.

His face broke in a wry smile. 'Did you want Irene and the others to come with us? I'll have you know that all those years of living with my wife's jealous rages made me into an accomplished liar.'

'Are you sure it wasn't your lies that made her jealous in the first place?' I said. He looked up at me with an expression of genuine surprise. And then something that has happened before with Christian and I happened again – our eyes met and we both laughed.

How strange it was to find myself laughing again. To tell the truth, I've almost forgotten what it felt like during the last couple of weeks because, what with one thing and another, there hasn't been much to laugh about. But here I was doing it again, and for no good reason at all. And once I'd started, I just couldn't stop – not even when Christian did and stood there looking at me strangely. To my horror I suddenly realized that my laughter had turned into tears. I turned away from him, searched through my handbag for some Kleenex, and blew my nose.

'I'm sorry,' I said.

'What for?'

'For making a fool of myself.'

There was a short pause. Then, 'You haven't made a fool of yourself at all,' he said in a deep, gentle voice.

I dried my eyes in my compact mirror, carefully wiping away the mascara which had smudged underneath, and then I turned back towards him with a watery smile.

'How about that drink?' he said. 'It looks like you need it even more than I do.'

I hesitated. 'Thank you but I can't,' I said at last. 'I must get home.'

'Must you?'

I shrugged. 'My husband is expecting me.'

'Come on, Gloria, think of yourself for a change! And if you can't do that, think of me. I could do with a bit of cheering up myself.'

Feeling like children bunking off school we crept into my car, which was parked just outside the pub where Irene and Melanie always go, and drove through a storm of fireworks to another one half a mile away – one of those yellow-brick modern places surrounded by large car-parks that you sometimes see on the edge of main roads. When Christian asked me what I wanted to drink, I was about to say an orange juice and then thought, What the hell, and ordered a brandy. So far have I fallen in so short a time, I reflected as I felt the first drop of its sweet heat slip down my throat – that I, Gloria Gold, a contented housewife who never used to drink much at all, am sitting drowning my sorrows in spirits in a public house!

'Well, tell me what's been going on,' Christian said as he lit the first of many cigarettes.

With a mouthful of brandy inside me, my bravado was returning. 'Nothing much,' I insisted brightly. 'I just had rather a difficult couple of weeks, that's all. I mean, first my sister's husband left her. And then I found out that my daughter is . . . that she's living with a . . . with a Nigerian. And,' I added as he opened his mouth, 'and I also found out that my son . . . that my son –' I stopped.

'Yes?' he said, leaning forward on his stool.

'That he's a homosexual,' I went on, forcing myself to

say the actual word. I hadn't said it out loud since the night Robert told us, not even to myself. Now, when I heard myself say it, I knew that I could never again pretend it wasn't true.

He sat back, his eyes wide with amazement. 'Bloody hell, Gloria!' he muttered under his breath. 'If that's what you call "rather a difficult couple of weeks" I'd hate to think what your really bad times are like.'

After that there was no stopping me – before I knew what was happening I had told him almost everything. And though at no time did he say he actually agreed with me about Benedict being unsuitable or the tragedy of Robert being 'gay', neither did he tell me I was being a prejudiced bigot, or that what I'd said and done was wrong. In fact, the only opinion he did express was straightforward concern for me: 'Oh, that must be hard for you,' he said over and over, and, 'Poor Gloria! I can imagine how that made you feel!'

Oh, the utter relief of having someone think of me for a change! Honestly, I could have talked to him for ever – which I very nearly did. Because before I knew what was happening a bell suddenly rang out from the back of the bar.

'What? That can't be the bell for last orders?' I screamed, jumping to my feet and knocking over a stool (I'm afraid I'd had three brandies by then). 'How could I have stayed so late? Morry must be frantic with worry. You'll have to excuse me, Christian, I've got to go.'

'So has everyone else,' he said with a smile. He stood up and handed me my overcoat. 'And,' he added firmly, taking my arm as I swayed out into the car-park, 'I'm going to drive you home.'

By the time we reached Hendon I had, thank goodness, sobered up a bit, and I was beginning to feel a little shame-faced. What on earth was I going to say to Morry, who'd probably spent the last few hours on the telephone, ringing the hospitals to find out if I'd been hit by a firework or involved in a car accident.

'Home, madam,' Christian said, switching off the ignition as we pulled up outside the house.

'Thank you, Jeeves,' I replied.

We sat there side by side in silence for a moment, staring through the windscreen. A rocket exploded at the end of the street, opening out above us in an umbrella of sparks. I turned towards Christian's profile and let out a long, relieved sigh. 'I can't thank you enough for this evening,' I said. 'I can't tell you how much better I feel just for having talked about things. But I've been so selfish, and I haven't asked how you are. Please forgive me.'

Now he sighed. 'There's nothing to forgive.' Then he took a deep breath and turned towards me and started to say something else. But after the first syllable he seemed to think better of it because he bit his lip. 'You'd better go in,' he said, opening his door.

I got out and he locked up, and handed me the keys. I opened the garden gate, then hesitated for a moment. 'If it isn't too late to ask, Christian, how are you?'

He shrugged. 'Oh, I'm okay.'

'Any news from your wife?'

He shook his head. 'To tell the truth, I'm beginning not to care. Out of sight, out of mind, I'm afraid.' He turned away and took a few steps down the street, then stopped and came back to me, and to my surprise gripped both my hands in his. 'You will be coming to class next week, won't you?' he said in an awkward, rather gruff voice.

'I promise.'

'Good,' he said. 'I look forward to it. Because I've missed you, Gloria.'

After that, he was gone in a flash, leaving me to ponder on what he'd said all the way to the front door. However, the moment I put my key in the lock, all thoughts about anything other than Morry fled from my mind. Because the downstairs lights were off, and so, when I walked in, were the upstairs lights as well. Was Morry walking the streets in search of me?

No, of course he wasn't: he was asleep in front of the television.

Oh well, what can one expect after thirty-six years of marriage?

It's nice to think that someone is looking forward to seeing me next week.

Saturday, 8th November

It is three o'clock in the afternoon and I'm lying in bed, writing this down with pencil and paper. I am in bed because I'm ill. First, I have a headache. Second, my heart is racing. Third, my mind has been infected by all that has happened in the past few weeks, and now spends its days charging off in foolish directions like a wild dog let off the leash. No use shouting 'Stay!' and 'Heel!', I've tried and it doesn't work. It seems that my mind has developed a mind of its own.

Suffice it to say that since I got up on Thursday morning, I have not been able to concentrate my thoughts on any subject bar one, and that – or rather he – is not the housework. Consequently, though I have managed to make the beds and sweep the kitchen floor every now and then, the rest of the cleaning still remains to be done. As for the large, well-stocked fridge which has been my pride and joy throughout my married life, it is empty but for a jar of pickled herrings, half a salami, four eggs, a bowl of chicken fat and a dried-up corner of Cheddar cheese. Oh, I have been out shopping – yesterday I even went to the supermarket. But while I was wheeling my trolley up and down the aisles, I began to feel dizzy. Suddenly I looked into the trolley and saw that I had filled it with packets of pork sausages, bacon, breaded scampi and deep-frozen prawns. There was even a fresh crab in there, lurking under a packet of cup-cakes. Good God, I thought, if I meet anyone I know they'll think I've undergone a Christian conversion! A hot flush of panic washed over me, and I'm afraid I abandoned the loaded trolley in the middle of the aisle and ran out into the street.

Hot flushes at my age! I thought I'd done with all of that with the menopause. It was a good thing none of the family were coming for dinner last night because, in the end, all Morry and I had to eat was wurst and eggs.

'Are you on strike?' he said, staring at me across the bare table-cloth.

I put down my knife and fork. 'No, Morry, I'm not on strike.'

He closed his newspaper and pushed it away from him. 'Then why no supper?'

'We've been married for thirty-six years,' I said. 'To my knowledge this is the first Friday night in all that time that you've not had a proper meal. Now, I ask you, be reasonable – is that any cause for complaint?'

'I'm not complaining,' he said defensively. 'I'm just asking if anything's the matter.'

'Of course something's the matter!' I snapped. 'Do I usually make wurst and eggs on Friday nights? Can't you see from my face that I'm ill?'

'Well, in that case shouldn't you see the doctor?' he said.

I laughed shortly. 'What can Dr Sheiner do for me? He can't help me – euthanasia's illegal.'

'Euthanasia? But . . .' He shook his head. 'It's not the children again?' I shrugged. 'Oh, Gloria,' he said. 'You can't stop living just because of what's happened.'

'I haven't stopped living,' I retorted angrily. 'All I've done is cook you wurst and eggs!'

Why, I wonder, has Morry been annoying me so much this week? He's constantly complaining, whatever I do or don't do. I bet Christian would never have complained if his second wife gave him wurst and eggs for dinner. Judging from what he told me about her, he'd have been grateful for anything.

Dear Christian. He's really such a marvellous person. I can't imagine why both his wives left him. I certainly wouldn't leave him if I were married to him. I don't think I've ever met a man who's quite so thoughtful and polite. And he seems to grow more and more good-looking the better you get to know him.

I do hope I didn't make too much of a fool of myself in the pub, talking so much about the children. I hope he wasn't bored. Morry clams up nowadays if I so much as mention Robert and Sharon. You'd think he'd be interested. After all, they're his children too. Yet Christian, who has never met them, is willing to talk about them for hours and hours. If only Morry was a little more like Christian, then . . .

There goes my mind again, running away in wild directions! I must stop it. I must . . . Oh Lord, I can hear footsteps coming upstairs. I'd better hide this notebook in case Morry sees what I've been writing.

*

That wasn't Morry, that was Sharon. Yes, I have just received a royal visitation from her, the substance of which has wiped all thoughts of Christian from my mind.

'Hallo, there,' she said, sticking her long, untidy mane of hair round the bedroom door. 'Dad said you're ill. What's the matter with you?'

'What should be the matter?' I said, shoving my notebook further under the covers and sticking the cold-pack Morry had brought me on my forehead. 'I've got a headache, that's what.'

'Oh, I'm sorry. Can I get you an aspirin?'

'An aspirin won't cure it. Well, don't stand there on the drafty landing, you'll catch pneumonia. Come on in.' And knowing how much she hates illness I added as I propped myself up on the pillows, 'Don't worry, what I've got isn't catching. To what do I owe the pleasure of your presence at home on a Saturday afternoon?'

She shrugged, and smiled brightly. 'I just thought I'd pop in and say hallo. I brought you some flowers.' She handed me a small vase overflowing with yellow freesia.

'Very nice,' I said, sniffing them suspiciously. What, I wondered, did she want from me? 'Put them out in the hall when you go, will you?'

'Don't you want them on the bedside table?'

'What, have flowers in a bedroom? Do you want to poison me?' I said. 'How many times do I have to tell you that flowers give out carbon monoxide?'

I handed her back the vase, which she put on the dressing-table. 'Actually, it's leaves that give out gas,' she said. 'And it's carbon dioxide, not monoxide, and then only at night. Plants actually give out oxygen during the day.'

What it is to have a daughter with a university education. A real *mavin*, she is. 'Just put the flowers outside

in the hall when you go, and don't argue, dear,' I said as
I turned the cold-pack.

'Do you want me to leave, then?'

'Of course not,' I muttered, closing my eyes.

'Good,' she said. 'Because I wanted to have a talk to
you.' I winced. What is it now? I thought as she sat
down on the end of my bed. 'You see, Mum, I'm seeing
someone.'

I sighed. 'I know you are,' I said, and reached for the
thermometer. Why did she think I was lying there feeling
so terrible?

'I don't mean Benedict,' she said. 'I'm seeing someone
else.'

I put the thermometer in my mouth. 'Is he a Nigerian,
too?' I mumbled, glancing at her through my half-closed
eyelids. She shook her head. 'He's not by any chance
Jewish?' I joked bitterly.

She smiled. 'As a matter of fact, he is.' I spat the
thermometer out, sat up, and threw the cold-pack on the
bedside table. 'But don't get the wrong idea,' she added
quickly. 'I don't see him in the sense you're thinking I
do.'

'How do you know what I'm thinking?' I said. 'You
tell me you're seeing someone. All I know is that. Why
should I care to know more? As you've told me often
enough, your life is your own, Sharon. So, tell me, are
you planning to marry him or what? What's his income?
Where does he live? What does he do for a living?'

Sharon shook her head sadly. 'He's a kind of doctor,
Mum.'

My face lit up. 'Why didn't you say? Darling! I'm
delighted! But, wait a minute! Does Benedict know you're
seeing him?' She nodded. I frowned. 'And he doesn't
mind?'

'Of course not,' she said. 'In fact, he introduced me to him. Actually, he sees him too. Sometimes we see him together.'

My blood ran cold. Suddenly I felt terrible again. 'Sharon,' I croaked. 'What kind of set-up is this? It sounds like something that you read in the *News of the World*! I mean, I know these Africans believe in polygamy, but . . .' Her face darkened like a stormy sky, and I knew that once again I'd managed to put my foot in it.

'You don't understand,' she said in a chilly voice. 'Benedict and I are his patients.'

At that moment I remembered what Robert had said about AIDS affecting heterosexuals, and my cold blood froze solid. 'What's the matter, darling?' I said, gripping her by the wrist. 'What are you telling me? That you're both ill?'

She pulled her wrist away. 'No, we're not ill,' she said impatiently. 'He's not that kind of a doctor. He's a psychotherapist.'

'What?'

'A psychotherapist,' she said. 'You've heard of Sigmund Freud, haven't you? Well, a kind of analyst. A shrink.'

'A shrink,' I murmured, leaning back on the pillows and giving her a long, curious stare. 'I see.' I have to say that for the first time in my life I felt afraid of my daughter. I mean, I've always known that she was funny in the head, especially since this Benedict business. But I never guessed just how funny in the head she was, and I never realized that she knew it too. I was shocked, I really was. However, after I'd thought about it for a moment it made quite a lot of sense to me, and all her peculiarities fell into place: her left-wing ideas; her dislike of fur coats; her decision to turn down the singles holiday in Israel we offered her as a twenty-first birthday present. No wonder I've always thought she was mad – she is mad. When she smiled at me next, I smiled back to humour her. 'Very nice, dear,' I said.

She raised her eyebrows as if she didn't believe me. 'Are you surprised I'm seeing someone?'

I hesitated. 'So so. Not really. I've known for a long time that you've had a few problems.' She nodded. 'And is this psychotherapist a help to you?' I asked guardedly.

'Yes, he's a great help.'

'Good, dear,' I said, growing braver. 'I only hope he finds a cure for you and Benedict.'

She laughed. 'Really, Mum, we're not looking for a "cure". We're not mad, you know.'

'No, dear. Of course you're not.'

'He's just someone we each go and talk to for an hour every week.'

'I see.'

'He helps us to see things more clearly, and to deal with our problems.'

'Well, I hope he makes you both see that this unsuitable relationship just can't go on much longer,' I couldn't help but add.

Her eyes flashed. 'Our relationship's not a problem,' she snapped.

Not for you, you selfish girl, I thought, but what about for me and your father? 'Of course not, darling!'

'No,' she said. 'The problem's more you.'

'Me?' I laughed. 'Sharon, what on earth are you talking about? How can I be your problem?'

'I feel you don't accept me as I am, Mum,' she said.

'Nonsense. What choice do I have? Do I ever interfere while you ruin your life? And do you ever listen to a word of advice I give?'

149

'That's what I mean,' she said. 'You're always trying to change me.'

'If I do, I'm only trying to bring you to your senses,' I said – and instantly regretted it. After all, under the circumstances, since she really is mad, it was not the most tactful remark to make. 'I'd like to talk to this doctor of yours,' I said more gently. 'I think I might be able to fill him in on a few details about your behaviour.'

Instead of looking angry as I imagined she might, she beamed at me with pleasure. 'Would you?' she said in a thrilled voice. 'Actually, that was exactly what I wanted to ask you. Will you come with me to see him next Friday?'

Thursday, 13th November

It is a good thing I am going with Sharon to see her doctor tomorrow. Because something is definitely wrong with my mind: I am beginning to imagine things about a certain person. First, in class last night I imagined he was looking at me all the time. Well, to be honest, I was doing most of the looking, but whenever I looked at him, he happened to be looking at me too, and our eyes met in an awkward collision which neither of us could escape from – like two cars locking bumpers in the High Street, with both drivers shunting backwards and forwards, struggling to get free. Second, I seemed to fancy that there was something deep and meaningful in his looks, which when I think about it in the cold light of day, certainly could not have been there. I mean, why should he look at me that way? I must be nearly ten years older than he is, and I am no Joan Collins. Even Morry no longer looks at me that way. He no longer looks at me any way, unless it is reproachfully.

'What?' he said last night as I put his supper down on the table before I went off to class. 'Not wurst and eggs again?'

'What's wrong with it?' I snapped. 'It used to be one of your favourite dishes.'

'Yes, but not every night of the week!'

'Don't exaggerate,' I said, sitting down beside him.

He picked up his knife and fork with a show of reluctance and shook his head. 'Six nights in a row you've given me wurst and eggs. What happened to all those wonderful meals you used to make? Soups and roasts and stews and goulashes? I'm turning into a piece of salami!'

'Honestly, Morry!' I shouted. 'What do you want – a seven-course dinner? I'm not running a restaurant. Go to McDonald's if you want a selection. I've got better things to do all day than sit around planning your meals!'

Now that I see those words written down, I can hardly believe that I said them. Never mind that I was so rude to Morry, what I said isn't even true. Because, actually, I haven't anything better to do than to plan his meals – except, of course, to write my autobiography, which I'm not doing, or to do the housework, which I don't seem to be doing much of any more, either.

I really must pull myself together. I know what – I'll scrub the house from top to bottom, then force myself to go to the supermarket and do a big shop. When I come home I'll spend the afternoon preparing something special for Morry's supper: soup, perhaps, followed by meat loaf and roast potatoes, with maybe a baked Alaska for dessert. After all, it really isn't fair to take it out on Morry because I feel . . . I feel . . . Oh Christian!

What has happened to my autobiography? I had planned to be half-way through Chapter Five – 'Maturity and Me' – by now. But how can I write about being mature when I don't feel mature at all? Not only that, I'm acting like an irresponsible teenager. I mean, when was the last time I had the family round for supper? I couldn't bear to, really I couldn't: we'd all sit around the table, staring at each other in silence – Angel and Ruth, Robert and Sharon, Morry and me. Because what could we talk about that wasn't either depressing or taboo? I certainly don't want the atmosphere ruined by any of Angel's talk about safe sex. That alone would be enough to give Morry indigestion. For this I should slave for hours over a hot stove? No wonder I can't face the thought of inviting them all.

I've just realized that I can't spend this afternoon cooking a special dinner for Morry. Because I agreed I'd meet Christian for lunch in the British Museum.

'I want to show you the King's Library,' he said when we were standing alone in the corridor after class last night.

'Why?' I said sceptically, staring at my fingernails. 'Do you think it'll inspire me to write like Shakespeare?'

He laughed. 'Who knows? Rubbing shoulders with all that great literature? We've got to do something to cure your writer's cramp.'

'I don't know why you don't just give up on me,' I said, as our eyes crashed in one of those collisions.

'Because I care about your writing and . . . well, because I like you, Gloria,' he said quietly. 'I like you very much.'

Pull yourself together, I warned myself, turning away as I felt a damned blush stain my cheeks crimson. I mean, why should I have been embarrassed when he probably says that to all his students? Why should I think I'm being singled out for special treatment when he probably takes all hopeless would-be writers to the British Museum? It doesn't mean a thing – just like it doesn't mean a thing that he insisted on paying for my tea-break tea. Didn't he pay for Melanie's tea, too? I didn't notice her blushing.

Perhaps if I got to the shops early enough this morning, I could buy something easy for Morry's dinner, which I could pop in the oven when I get home.

No, I've no time for any food shopping: I've just looked at myself in the wardrobe mirror, and I'm sorry to say my hair looks terrible. I'll have to phone Mario and see if he can fit me in this morning for a tint and a restyle. Surely Morry won't mind if there's wurst and eggs for supper just once more?

Later . . .

What can I possibly write down about what happened this afternoon between me and Christian? I shouldn't really write down a single word. Because if Morry, God forbid, turned on this machine and instead of loading in his bank records loaded in this file by mistake, he'd find out what went on behind one of the postage-stamp cabinets in the King's Library. And then what? Would he throw me out of the house? Might my thirty-six-year marriage end in a divorce?

I doubt it. Knowing Morry, he'd probably presume that the 'I' I'd written about was the heroine of some short story and not me at all. Because Morry is probably incapable of imagining that I, Gloria Gold, his wife, am the sort of woman whom a man might want to kiss.

My hands are shaking so much I can hardly type a word of this. My tummy feels all fizzy and excited – just like it does after a glass of champagne. Yet all that I've had to drink since breakfast is one cup of coffee. For the first time in my life I've completely lost my appetite. I don't think I'll ever be able to eat again.

Oh, what a day! To think that when I woke up this morning I had no idea this was going to happen! All I thought was, he doesn't like you, stupid, all these funny looks and things are all in your silly head. But they weren't just in my head. He does like me. He said so. Not only that, but he has liked me for weeks.

Why me? That's what I don't understand. As I said to him after he first kissed me, why not someone else in the class – say, Irene or Melanie Thatcher who are both much younger and prettier than I am. 'Ours not to reason why,' he murmured in my ear, meanwhile running his fingers through my hair.

'Well,' I said, pulling away from him and smoothing down Mario's ruined set. 'I hope it's not going to be "Ours but to do and die"!'

He laughed and, taking hold of my hands, pulled me back towards him. 'So, you've got quite a literary mind after all, Gloria Gold!' he grinned.

'Oh, I learned that old thing at school.'

His smile faded and his face grew serious. 'Oh Gloria,' he sighed softly, looking down at me with his gorgeous sea-green eyes. 'You know, I've wanted to kiss you for ages.'

'Have you?' I gulped.

He nodded. 'Ever since we had lunch together in Golders Green.'

This isn't happening, I told myself as his stubbly chin drew closer and he kissed me again, this really isn't happening. It had to be some sort of fantasy, a crazy dream. Yet if it was a dream, it was one I had no desire to wake up from. Because frankly I was enjoying myself more than I could remember doing in a long time. If my mind was asleep, my body felt as if it was waking up from a heavy, drug-induced slumber. How long had it been dozing?

Fifteen years? Twenty? Suddenly it felt fully alive again: tickles and prickles ran up and down my spine, and a great warmth was flooding through me. Oh, it was wonderful! For a moment I was lost in it. And then, suddenly . . .

'Stop!' I said, pulling away from him.

'What's the matter?'

'Well, I'm a married woman and you're a married man! We shouldn't be doing this! Certainly not in the middle of the British Museum!'

A seductive expression crept over his face. 'We can always go to my flat,' he said. 'It's not far from here, about a mile away in Clerkenwell.' And then, seeing how shocked I looked, he laughed. 'Only joking, Gloria. And don't be afraid. You're not committing yourself to anything. After all, we haven't done anything – we've only kissed.'

Maybe it was only a kiss to him. For all I know he does that sort of thing every day. But for me . . . Why, I haven't kissed anybody but Morry that way since the day I was married. To me, it already felt like I'd committed adultery, right there in the King's Library. On reflection, however, I see that Christian was right: you can hardly call it 'committing adultery' after one kiss.

Well, it was more than one kiss by that stage, it was probably two or three. By the time we parted at Holborn tube station at four o'clock, I'm embarrassed to say that I'd lost count of the number. All I know is that I was enjoying them more and more, so much so that I wanted them to go on and on and on . . .

Morry will be home soon, and I'm beginning to feel terrible. How could I have let such a thing happen? To kiss a man – and in public! That isn't like me. In fact, it's the kind of thing I'd be shocked at if I heard that somebody else had done it. How could I have let it happen? Perhaps I'll be able to understand it better if I go through it in my mind again.

The moment we'd said our initial 'hallos' under the Museum's grand portico, the strange awkwardness I'd felt last night came down between us like a heavy curtain. Making stilted small-talk, we walked into the library, and he showed me some examples of early printing techniques. Truthfully, I was so aware of his hand resting on my arm, guiding me, that I hardly knew what I was seeing. Just when the tension between us was so great that I had almost decided to leave, he pulled me behind a high wooden cupboard made up of funny narrow vertical drawers – a stamp cabinet, as I later found out – put his arms around me, and drew me towards him in what seemed like an ever-lasting embrace.

That is the whole, unadulterated adulterous story. It makes me shiver just to think of it again. It does not, however, make me any clearer as to why it happened. Why should he like me?

'Because you're warm and funny,' he volunteered when I asked him this very question while we were having a coffee in the cafeteria half an hour after our first embrace. 'Hasn't anyone ever told you what a terrific sense of humour you have?'

I gave this question some thought for all of two seconds. 'Not for the past thirty-six years,' I said. 'Oh, except my friend Claudia. But then, she only thinks I'm being funny when I'm not.'

He took my hand across the table, and rubbed his palm slowly against mine. How strange my small fingers looked against his large, stubby ones! However, his touch didn't feel strange, it felt perfectly familiar – just like our conversation had been ever since the moment we'd kissed. I have a feeling that Christian was thinking this, too, because his face became suddenly serious again.

'I really like you, Gloria,' he murmured.

How can he? I thought. Why, he doesn't even know me. He should see me in the morning, in my dressing-gown and slippers, scrubbing the kitchen sink. 'You should know me better,' I said.

'I'd like to,' he replied. 'I really would. When can I see you again?'

Naturally I told him it was out of the question for us ever to be alone together any more, and after a protracted discussion on the subject – punctuated by more kisses, I'm ashamed to say – I said that I'd go to the pub with him after class next Wednesday to explain why we cannot go on meeting like this. Not that I need to explain. After all, it's self-evident, isn't it? I mean, I'm just not the sort of person who does this kind of thing.

Oh no! A car's just drawn up outside. Can that be Morry? Yes, I've just looked out of the window and it certainly is. How can I face him after what's happened? And oh, what'll he say when he finds out it's wurst and eggs for supper again? What reasonable excuse can I possibly give?

Friday, 14th November

Down to earth today with a horrible bang. The British Museum seems a thousand light years away from where I have been – visiting Sharon's psychotherapist. No wonder people called them 'shrinks' – never in my life have I felt so small. To think that you pay them good money, just to have them sit there and make you squirm.

I met Sharon outside the big, white-washed house in Belsize Park where this Dr Kleinholtz works. She gave a peculiar, grateful smile when she saw me, and even touched me on the arm – a very uncharacteristic gesture which made me wonder what I was letting myself in for.

She rang the bell, a buzzer sounded, and the door opened by itself. 'What, no receptionist?' I said as we walked into an unswept hallway full of unopened post and half-dead, straggly plants. 'What kind of surgery is this?'

'It isn't a surgery, Mum. It's a consulting room.'

I ran a finger along the hall table, and grimaced as I examined the trail in the dust, then followed her into a small side-room, in which there were two shabby-looking armchairs and a wall of bookshelves, scattered with more plants, some of which had shed their leaves on the carpet. 'Doesn't he have a cleaner, either?' I remarked pointedly.

Sharon sank down on one of the chairs as if she was exhausted. 'For heaven's sake, what does it matter?'

I looked at her angrily. 'There's no need to use that patronizing tone with me. I may be your mother but I'm not a fool. Surely it's not too much to ask that a doctor's waiting-room be clean.'

'He's not a proper doctor – not in the medical sense,' she murmured.

'What are you telling me? That he's untrained? That he's a crank? I suppose he prescribes brown rice instead of antibiotics?' She laughed. 'What's so funny?' I asked.

'You are. And I can't believe you don't know it.' That made me think of Christian, of course, and what he'd said yesterday about my sense of humour. My head began to spin with thoughts of him, of the warmth of his cheek against mine, of the rough texture of his hair.

Sharon sighed. 'Look, why don't you sit down and relax.'

mistaking that he was Jewish, and in a distinguished way
he was quite handsome, and he was a doctor (of a sort),
and from the way they were smiling at each other it was
obvious that he and Sharon liked each other quite a bit.
A pity that he isn't a few years younger, I reflected,
because, really, at a pinch, he might do as a husband for
her. Mind you, he'd have to be more than a few years
younger – say thirty or forty years at the least. Still . . .
could a man his age father grandchildren? That, after all,
was the important question because now I know that
Robert won't be getting married, well, Sharon's my only
chance at being a grandmother, isn't she?

My thoughts came to an abrupt halt when I saw the
suspicious look that Sharon was giving me. 'What are you
thinking?' she asked.

'Nothing,' I said hurriedly.

'Come off it,' she said coldly. 'You were sizing up Dr
Kleinholtz as a possible husband for me, weren't you?'

'Sharon!' I expostulated. 'What a ridiculous thing to
say. How absolutely . . . well, it's ridiculous, isn't it?'
Here I appealed to Dr Kleinholtz, but he didn't bat an
eyelid. 'Whatever makes you think such a thing?' I said,
turning back to her.

'Because you're always doing it,' she said. 'Don't deny
it. I've watched you ever since my thirteenth birthday
party, when I saw the way you looked at Robert's friends.
You're so obvious when you do it – you get a special,
calculating expression in your eyes.'

They say that madmen develop extraordinary powers.
Unfortunately for me, Sharon's had turned out to be
mind-reading. And even more unfortunately, it appeared
she'd had these powers since she'd turned thirteen. 'Be a
dear,' I said. 'You're embarrassing the doctor.'

Dr Kleinholtz raised the head that had momentarily

'I don't want to sit down, thank you very much,' I said.
'And I am relaxed.'

'So I can see.'

I looked at my watch. It was just five-past one. I found
myself wondering suddenly what Christian was doing.
Yesterday, at this precise moment, he had been kissing
me in the British Museum. Was he in the pub now? Or
hard at work on his new novel? Could he – no, I was sure
he wasn't – but oh, could he possibly be thinking of me?
He had probably forgotten all about our kiss already – if
he was not regretting it – but I felt the touch of his lips
still, like a burn on my face. I touched my cheek now,
and my own lips, and wondered how it was that both
Morry and Sharon could have failed to notice that something so momentous had happened to me.

'Half of these books are in German,' I remarked, glancing suspiciously at the shelves. 'Is this Dr Kleinholtz a
Nazi?'

'As I told you last week, he's Jewish,' she said impatiently. 'In fact, if you must know, I think he was a
refugee from Nazi persecution. Now for God's sake relax
and sit down.'

'I am relaxed. I told you before I was. It seems to me
that you're the one who's on edge.'

'I'm not!' she countered. 'You are!'

'No I'm not!' I retorted. And then I thought to myself,
Here we go again, round and round in a big circle of
accusation and denial, like two people on opposite sides
of a runaway merry-go-round who can't get off. Why
can't things ever be simple and open between us? I mean,
why couldn't we both admit then and there that we were
apprehensive about what this doctor might diagnose?

Why must Sharon and I always lie to each other? How
did that dear little girl in pig-tails and her adoring mother

come to this snarling state of affairs? Why, I still clearly remember the moment she was born, and my secret joy that she was not the son that Morry was longing for but the daughter I wanted for myself! A son you lose when he grows up, I remember thinking, but a daughter remains a friend for life. Oh dear, if only I'd known then what I know now!

Determined to make more effort to get on with her, I sat down and said, 'Well, isn't this nice?'

She gave me an uncomprehending frown. 'How do you mean?'

I smiled. 'You and I, spending lunch together on a weekday. Why, we haven't done this for years – not since you started that job in television. I tell you what, we can go up to Hampstead afterwards, and have a bite to eat. Wouldn't that be nice?'

'Very nice,' she said without enthusiasm. 'But I can't come. I've got to get back to work.'

'So soon, dear? What kind of job is this, that you don't have time to have lunch with your mother?'

'I'll have been gone nearly two hours by the time I get back as it is. You know, Mum, it isn't easy for me to get away to come here. Oh, for heaven's sake, don't look so upset. I'm sorry I can't come, but that's how it is.'

How many times have I heard that girl say she's sorry without sounding like she is in the slightest? Could I help it if, when I next spoke, I sounded aggrieved? 'Well, if you can take the time off to come here and talk to this doctor-who-isn't-a-doctor whenever you feel like it, how come you can't take time off to have coffee with me?'

She took a deep breath. 'It's a question of priorities,' she said.

'Clearly!'

160

'And I don't come whenever I feel like it,' 'I only come once a week.'

'Just tell me this – when was the last time for coffee together? Why, it must have been

'Oh for God's sake –' she began. And buzzer sounded in the hall and she jumped 'That means he's ready for us. Let's go.'

The consulting room was more like a and a very large, high-ceilinged one at with all sorts of books, plants and over-st furniture. Winter sunlight blazed through windows at the far end, and in front of sort of desk half-obscured by yet more glad to meet you, Doctor,' I said, advanc with my hand held out, ready to make a 'Anyone who might be able to help Shar of as a family friend.'

'Good afternoon, Mrs Gold,' a quiet close behind me, making me jump rig I swivelled round, and saw a tiny w with a face like a wizened apple sittin brown leather chair. To my surprise, and take the hand I had offered, b own, disproportionately large palm dismissive gesture motioned me towa which were situated a few feet away uncertainly beside one until Sharo down in the other.

'Hallo Sharon,' he said.

She smiled back warmly at him: this exchange with raised eyebro myself, they were on first name t cases of women falling in love with I looked at him with new eye

161

fallen on to his chest. 'Mrs Gold,' he said. 'Let me assure you that there is very little that embarrasses me. But you, Mrs Gold, you are blushing.'

'Are you sure? I don't know why. I mean, I'm not embarrassed.' He continued to stare at me blankly while the traitorous burning flush spread up my cheeks. 'I mean, if what Sharon said isn't true, why should I be embarrassed?'

He raised his eyebrows questioningly. 'Why should you be?' he repeated.

And before I knew what I was doing, I had started to answer him. 'Because . . . because . . .' I looked away from his mesmerizing gaze and swallowed hard. 'Truthfully, yes, I am embarrassed, Doctor,' I admitted. 'I mean, this is a delicate business for me. In your line of work you are probably used to . . . to people with problems like Sharon has. But for me it's different. You see, this is the first time we've ever had this sort of thing in the family.'

'By which you mean . . .?'

I was taken aback. 'Well, I . . . Surely that's for you to tell me. I mean, I'm not the doctor, you are.' I glanced at my daughter who was looking at me with intensity, and noticed for the first time that she had put on a suit to come here, and tied back her untidy hair. Obviously, she was trying to make a good impression. My heart melted. 'Of course I don't mean that my Sharon is mad, of course not. At least I didn't think so until . . . But she's seeing you, isn't she, doctor? So there must be something wrong with her. I do think – how shall I put it – that she's gone a little off the rails.'

'Off the rails,' he echoed.

'Yes,' I said, my nervousness slowly subsiding. 'You know what I mean. When a nice, attractive girl like Sharon reaches the age of thirty-four without once expressing the desire to get married, and then her parents find out she's been lying to them – when, as I'm sure you realize, Doctor, they only have her best interests at heart – well, that she's been lying to them for God knows how many months –'

Here Sharon interrupted me. 'Eighteen, if you must know.'

I gasped. 'Eighteen months? You've been seeing Benedict as long as that?'

'Living with him,' she corrected me.

I looked at the doctor. 'You see? For eighteen months she's been living a life of deception, pretending that her "flatmate" was her flatmate, when in reality he was something completely different, and on top of that, an extremely unsuitable man! Well, now, she may not be mad, but that's not normal behaviour for a girl of her age, is it? What am I supposed to think?'

There was a long pause, during which Sharon coughed once and Dr Kleinholtz did nothing but continue to stare at me blankly. Eventually I went on, 'The thing is, whenever I so much as say a word to her, which isn't very often, well, she immediately jumps down my throat and tells me to mind my own business. As if it wasn't my business. She just can't seem to see that it is. I'm her mother, so of course her welfare is my business. Isn't that so, Doctor Kleinholtz?' I waited for him to reply, but still he said nothing. 'However, my Sharon doesn't seem to understand this. How can she understand it when she's never had children of her own – and maybe never will, unless . . . You understand what I mean, though. Don't you, Doctor? I mean, I suppose you're a father? Hmm?'

Silence.

I cleared my throat and asked again. 'Um, do you have children, Dr Kleinholtz?'

There was another long pause, during which I began to feel stupid. 'He won't answer you, Mum,' said Sharon softly, leaning back in her chair. 'He can't tell you anything about himself.'

'Why not?' I asked. I frowned from one to the other. 'I've been telling him about myself!'

'Whether or not he's a father is irrelevant –'

'Not to me!' I interrupted her.

'Irrelevant to us, and to our situation,' she finished firmly. 'In fact, it wouldn't help you to know.'

'I'll be the judge of that. And don't answer for other people. He can speak for himself.'

Could he? I was beginning to wonder. Because although we'd been there for ages, he'd hardly said a word. However, now he had decided to speak. At last! I thought as he uncrossed his legs and cleared his throat. I leaned forward expectantly as his lips parted. 'My Sharon,' I thought he said.

'Pardon?'

'My Sharon,' he repeated. Frowning at him, I sat back in the chair. 'You called your daughter "my Sharon",' he continued in the same flat, expressionless voice.

'When?' I said.

'Just now.'

'Did I?'

He nodded. 'Several times.'

Out of the corner of my eye I saw Sharon sit up and glance excitedly between us.

I shrugged. 'Funny,' I said. 'I can't remember.' He raised his white feathery eyebrows again. 'Why did you say that?' I asked. He stayed silent, so I went on, 'Are you telling me there's something wrong with my saying that – in saying "my Sharon"?'

'I was merely remarking on the use of the possessive pronoun.'

'As in "my" car, "my" hairbrush, "my" daughter,' Sharon muttered.

I looked down at my skirt, and noticed with dismay that there was a small stain on it. 'Well, you are my daughter,' I murmured as I scratched at it with a fingernail.

'Yes, Mum,' Sharon said gently. 'But I'm also a grown-up human being with a life of my own.'

And then it dawned on me. 'I see!' I said, looking up at the doctor. 'You're insinuating that I'm a possessive mother. Well, let me make one thing clear to you – I certainly am not. If Sharon's told you otherwise, it's a lie. Why, she left home years ago! And I've never interfered. Why, I don't even know what she's doing most of the time.'

Sharon whistled softly. 'Oh, come off it, Mum,' she said. 'You ring me at least twice every day, trying to keep tabs on me. Once, when I didn't answer the phone at seven-thirty in the morning, you even got the ex-directory operator to send round the police!'

'What else was I to do? For all I knew, you'd been murdered in your sleep, or tied up and raped by some robber. If you had been tied up, you would have been pleased! Believe me, Doctor, I was frantic. I would have gone round to her flat myself to see that she was all right, only she wouldn't let me know her address, and neither would the operator. Which is another thing – for a daughter not to tell her mother where she's living! Now, you must admit that's more than a little strange.'

He admitted nothing – he simply uncrossed his legs and brushed back his snow-white hair. After a long pause he moved his gaze from me to Sharon, who, in a state of great agitation, started to speak.

'Look, Mum, I know you mean well . . .'

'Of course I do. Believe me, my only concern in life is to see you happy.'

'But . . .' Here it comes, I thought, the qualifying 'but' that negates anything good she may ever say about me. 'But seriously, isn't it time you let go of me and let me lead my own life?'

'Tell me, have I ever stopped you doing what you wanted to do?' I protested. 'Just look at the way you live – in Kentish Town, in sin with that –'

'Mum, don't you dare call Benedict a –'

Here the doctor interrupted us by lifting his large hand. 'Let us see if we can keep things in perspective, so that we can make the most of our time together,' he said in his expressionless voice. I nodded, shot a disapproving look at Sharon, and then smiled at him. 'Mrs Gold,' he continued. 'It seems to me that Sharon does have a point here, when she talks of you "letting go" of her. After all, although your child, she's not a child any more, she's a 34-year-old woman.'

'Well, I wish she'd behave as if she was, Doctor,' I said. 'Believe me, if she did, I'd never say a word to her. As it is, I have no choice but to try and make her come to her senses.'

'Can't you see, Mum, that you can't just let go of me when I'm living the way you want me to? You have to let go now, and let me live the way I want to live. And with whom I want to live. I'm old enough to make my own decisions. And if I make a mistake or two along the way, so what? They'll be my own mistakes, and they won't kill me.'

But they'll kill me, I thought. 'Look, Sharon,' I reasoned. 'You love Robert, don't you? Well, if you saw him driving off the edge of a cliff, would you try to stop him, or would you let him go ahead?'

As soon as I'd said this, my heart fell into my stomach. Because, of course, my darling Robert is driving off the edge of a cliff, metaphorically speaking, and Sharon is not only not stopping him, but from what I can gather she is actively egging him on. I closed my eyes, and in my mind I saw a car with both my children in it toppling over Beachy Head. And there I was, standing by with my hands tied, powerless to stop them! Before I knew what was happening I had burst into tears.

Instead of coming over to comfort me or passing me a tissue, Dr Kleinholtz clasped his hands under his chin and sat there watching me in the most unsympathetic manner. Eventually, after I'd stopped crying and blown my nose, he said in a flat voice, 'It seems to me that you're upset.'

Brilliant, I thought. For this he calls himself a specialist and charges money? 'Of course I'm upset,' I snapped. 'Wouldn't you be if your only daughter was wasting her last chance of happiness, and your only son . . . your son . . .'

My voice trailed away. There was another pause. Dr Kleinholtz raised a bushy eyebrow. 'Your son?' he echoed.

I sniffed back my tears. 'Nothing,' I said. The doctor leaned forward, as if he expected me to speak. I smiled. 'I'm quite all right now, thank you,' I went on, hoping this would shut him up. But, nosey-parker that he was, he was not satisfied.

'Your son?' he repeated.

I took a deep breath. 'There's nothing wrong with my son.'

'Mum, Franz knows all about Robert.'

'How?'

'I told him, of course.'

'Really, it's not the sort of thing we want to spread around!'

'Why not?' she said, just as I expected her to. 'Being gay is nothing to be ashamed of. Anyway, Robert's my brother, and telling Franz isn't exactly what I'd call "spreading it around". He's my psychotherapist. I tell him everything.'

Everything? I thought with a surge of excitement. Why, if I could only get him on my own for a while, what could I not find out from him? Sharon, unfortunately, must have been using her mind-reading powers, because she added quickly, 'And anything that's said in this room is completely confidential.'

There was yet another short silence, and then the master of understatement chose to speak again. 'I wonder if talking about your son's homosexuality upsets you, Mrs Gold?'

If he's only wondering, I thought, then he shouldn't be in that chair – he ought to be sitting where Sharon is. 'I'm not here to talk about my son, Doctor,' I said. 'I'm here to discuss Sharon.'

'And Sharon, what do you feel about this?'

Sharon bit her lip for a moment, then cupped her chin in her hand thoughtfully. 'Well, I do feel that Robert is part of the problem – Mum's problem. But as far as I'm concerned, I suppose what upsets me is that I feel she has so little idea of me, what I'm really like as a person, what my feelings are, and my needs. So naturally part of me feels angry about this, and hurt, and upset because I'd like her to respect me. Yet I also feel . . . well, I feel that she has to worry about her children, because worrying about us makes up for inadequacies in her own life and her marriage – inadequacies that she can't bear to face.'

At this point I could no longer contain myself. 'Really, Sharon!' I burst out. 'You feel this, you feel that! If you ask me, that's half the problem – you feel too much and think too little. Why don't you use your head? I tell you why not – because if you thought things through, you'd see that the way you live just isn't sensible!'

This was getting too much for me. I was beginning to feel quite ill, and I flopped back in the chair, unable to move. 'Well, Doctor,' I sighed, smiling at him weakly. 'We've been here for quite some time now, and we've got nowhere at all as far as I can see. Now you begin to see the extent of the problem. Tell me honestly, can you do anything about all this?'

He looked at Sharon blankly, and then turned his gaze on me. 'I might be able to,' he said.

Honestly, those were the last words I'd expected to hear. I sat up, suddenly filled with new hope. 'You might?' I breathed.

'But it will take perseverance. And I'm afraid that in my line of work, Mrs Gold, perseverance doesn't come cheap.'

I shook my head. 'We're not rich people, Doctor, but whatever it's going to cost, my husband and I will find the money somewhere. Believe me, I'd pay any price to make my daughter happy.'

'I don't doubt your word, Mrs Gold,' he said. 'So that's settled then. I'll need to see you at least twice a week.'

'See me?' I gasped. 'What for? I think there's some mistake, Doctor – it's Sharon, not me, who needs the cure!'

Of course, I'm not going back there. What, pay money to be insulted again? Because he was insulting me, that's as clear as day is day. Because the implication is that it's my fault that Sharon is living with Benedict. And I suppose, by logical extension, it's my fault that Robert's 'gay'. And, if I asked him he'd probably say that it's also my fault that Morry spends all his time reading. I suspect there's a golden rule to psychotherapy – if it's at all possible, blame it on a wife-and-mother. Well, I won't take the blame, I won't. I've done my best. It's not my fault if everyone misinterprets what I do. No one appreciates me – except Christian. Oh Christian, Christian, if only Morry and the children were more like you!

Saturday, 15th November

As if yesterday wasn't enough for a woman! I had three phone calls this morning to end all phone calls.

The first one came when Morry was out having the car cleaned. I picked up the receiver only to hear a long silence. 'Hallo?' I said. 'Hallo?' Then I heard deep breathing. A sex maniac, I thought. 'You should be ashamed of yourself!' I shouted in disgust. 'At this hour of a Saturday morning!' The caller said nothing, just kept on breathing so I told him off again and started to put the phone down. But then a woman's voice cried, 'Wait! Is that Mrs Gold?'

'Who wants her?' I asked suspiciously.

There was a long pause in which I heard her blow her nose. 'That is you, isn't it? You don't know me. My name is Anne Green. I'm Peter's mother.'

'Whose mother?'

'Peter's,' she said. 'Surely you know who he is, don't you, Mrs Gold? I mean, hasn't your son told you?' She cleared her throat, then her voice came back in a whisper: 'My son Peter . . . and your son Robert. Well, they are . . . you know, making a home together.'

As I sat there in a stunned silence with a whirlwind of emotions rushing around inside me, the deep breathing started up again. It was then I realized that she was not breathing but weeping into the receiver. That started me off. For a full five minutes I sat there sobbing into the mouthpiece while she sobbed into my ear. When we'd both cried ourselves out, we blew our noses and dried our tears.

'I don't know what to say,' I said.

'Neither do I.'

We both sniffed a little to fill the awkward silence. Then,

'I never thought . . .' we both said in unison. We stopped.

'Please go on,' I said.

'No, no. I wouldn't dream of it,' she said politely. 'You first.'

'No, no, I insist,' I said. 'After all, you're the one who telephoned me.'

'I was only going to say, I never dreamed I'd ever have to make a phone-call like this.'

'Funny,' I said. 'That's just what I was going to say.'

'I mean, I thought I might one day have to ring up Peter's future in-laws. But this . . . this . . .' Her voice tailed off.

'I know,' I said. 'I can tell you, it's come as a dreadful shock to my husband and me.'

'It's been exactly the same with us as well. I haven't stopped crying since Peter told us a few weeks ago.'

'Funny, Robert told us a few weeks ago, too. Didn't you know before about him being . . . being a . . .' I forced myself to say the word, 'a homosexual?'

'No. Of course I knew he didn't have a special girlfriend or anything, but to tell you the truth, that never bothered me. I must have been blind not to have suspected something. But you see, he's not been living at home for years.'

'Oh?'

'Yes, he's been in the hospital.'

My heart stopped. 'Why? Is he sick?'

'No, no. He's a doctor.'

'A doctor?' I said curiously. Robert had not mentioned that.

'Yes,' she said. 'He's training to be a specialist.'

'Oh?' I said. For some strange reason, my spirits lifted. 'How old is he?'

'Twenty-seven.'

I gasped. Three years younger than Robert and training to be a specialist! The vision I'd had of the dirty old man in a raincoat who had corrupted Robert was forever banished from my mind.

On the other end of the receiver, his mother sighed again. 'I can't understand it,' she said. 'I mean, he was always such a quiet young man. And now this has happened. I keep asking myself over and over again, where did we go wrong?'

'Me too,' I said.

'I thought we'd brought him up so well.'

'Me too.'

'We even managed to put him through private school.' Here her voice changed, and suddenly became hostile. 'What I'm trying to say, Mrs Gold, is this: *we* did *our* best.'

'Do you think I didn't do my best?' I said with a touch of annoyance. 'You think we scrimped on Robert's education?'

'Robert's older than Peter, isn't he?' she said pointedly.

'He's thirty,' I said. 'So?'

'You'd think a man would know better at his age.'

My hackles rose. 'I'll have you know that my boy was never mixed up in anything like this before he met your son,' I said angrily.

'Well, neither was Peter. And I've got no idea what kind of person this Robert is.'

'He's wonderful,' I said without hesitation. 'He's clever, he's kind, he's been a model son. I've always said to Morry that any girl would be lucky to catch him.' She'd have to be very lucky indeed given the present circumstances, I thought to myself with a flash of bitterness.

'What exactly does he do for a living?' she asked after a short pause.

'He's an accountant.'

'Oh,' she said.

'And he's very successful,' I added.

'Oh?'

'Yes,' I went on. 'He works for an advertising agency. They've just bought him a BMW.'

'Oh?' I could hear by her tone that she was impressed. 'Very nice, too,' she said. 'Of course, Peter doesn't have much money, seeing as he's still training. My husband and I aren't rich people.' She cleared her throat, and when she next spoke, she sounded accusing. 'We always brought him up to know the value of money, but more than that, to value money less than other things.'

'I'll have you know, Mrs Green, that I brought up Robert that way, too. Do you think we're rich? And there's my daughter Sharon to think of, too.'

'How old is your daughter, Mrs Gold?'

'Thirty-four.'

'And I suppose that she's married?'

I hesitated. 'Not exactly.'

There was a long silence on the other end of the phone. 'She's not by any chance that way too?'

'Good God, no!' I gasped.

'I hope you don't mind me asking,' she said. 'You see, all of this is a bit new to me. And when you said she was thirty-four and not married I wondered if homosexuality might run in families, like diabetes or heart disease.'

You'll give me heart disease in a minute, I thought, if you come out with anything else like that. 'Let me assure you that my Sharon's completely normal,' I said. Which, although not quite true, went a long way to reassuring Mrs Green. But did it reassure me? Since she said it, I haven't stopped worrying that homosexuality is hereditary. Because if it is, that means that Robert's caught it from either Morry or me. Which must mean . . . 'How did you get my number?' I asked suddenly.

'I got it from Peter's address book when he wasn't looking,' she confessed. For this alone one had to admire her. 'I hope you don't mind me phoning you up,' she added. 'But when Peter told me he intended to move in with this . . . this man, I didn't know what to do. I thought, do I just sit back and allow this to happen, or do I try to do something about it?'

'I understand perfectly. I feel the same way. But what can you do?'

'I don't know,' she said glumly. 'Perhaps we could meet and discuss it.'

I thought about it for a moment. 'If you think it'd be any use,' I said eventually.

'There's no harm in trying, is there? Things couldn't be worse than they are.'

'I suppose not.' I wiped away a tear.

'Well,' she said. 'How about it?'

I pulled myself together. 'I'm game if you are. When shall we meet?'

'Any time. There's no emergency. How about this afternoon?'

'What are you doing for lunch?'

'Nothing. Why don't you come over to my house? I'll make us a snack.'

I hesitated. Much as I was interested in seeing what kind of family this friend of Robert's comes from, I was rather apprehensive about eating in an unknown woman's house. What would I say if she served me shell-fish or pork? 'Perhaps it'd be better to meet in town,' I suggested tactfully. 'I mean, for all we know we live miles apart. I live in Hendon. Where are you?'

'East Finchley.'

'Oh? Whereabouts?'

'Huntingdon Avenue. It's a little street behind the shops. Just behind the . . .' Now she hesitated.

'Yes?'

'Behind a big, rather ugly building. A sort of – um – church.'

My heart swelled with anger at her scathing tone. Well, I wasn't going to let her get away with that! 'That building isn't ugly. And it's not a church, it's a synagogue,' I said clearly.

'Oh? Do you know it?' she asked.

'I should do,' I said. 'I've been a member of it for the past twenty years.'

There was a long, shocked silence. 'Does that mean you're Jewish, Mrs Gold?' she gasped.

'Yes, I am. And, what's more, I'm proud of the fact,' I shouted.

'And so, Mrs Gold, am I.'

Now it was my turn to be speechless. 'Don't tell me you're Jewish too, Mrs Green?' I gasped.

'Enough with the formalities, Mrs Gold! Just call me Anne.'

'And please call me Gloria, Mrs Green.'

No sooner had I put the phone down than it rang

again. 'Hallo?' I said. My answer was another silence. I prayed it wasn't Benedict's mother asking if we could meet too, because, to tell the truth, two mothers in one day would have been too much for me. But no, after a long pause, a gruff man's voice asked if he'd got the right number, and when I said he had, he asked to speak to Mrs Gold.

'Speaking.'

His voice lowered to a sexy whisper: 'Hallo Gloria.'

I caught my breath. It was Christian. 'Hallo,' I whispered back. 'What are you doing, phoning me at home?'

'I had to,' he said. 'I needed to speak to you.'

'Why?'

'Well, because I've missed you since Thursday.'

At the mere mention of Thursday a great warmth flooded through me. 'Have you?' I croaked.

'Mmmm. Can you talk now? Or is somebody with you.'

'No. Morry's gone to the car-wash. I'm all alone.'

'So why are you whispering?'

I uncupped my hand from the mouthpiece and laughed. 'I really don't know.'

He laughed, too, then sighed deeply. 'Oh, I feel better just for hearing your voice, darling.'

'In that case you must be crazy.'

'Yes, I am crazy,' he said. 'I'm crazy about you.'

'Oh Christian! What a line you spin! You ought to use it in a book!'

'Just testing it out.'

We prattled on like overgrown children for five or six minutes, by the end of which I'd completely forgotten about Peter's mother's call. Suddenly I heard a car draw up outside and reality dawned. 'Morry's just come home,' I said. 'I've got to ring off.'

'Oh,' he pleaded. 'Just talk to me for one more minute.'

'I can't,' I whispered. 'I must go.'

'Gloria,' he said. 'Wait . . .'

The key turned in the latch, and Morry came marching in, a sheaf of magazines tucked into his armpit. A deep red blush was spreading up my cheeks, and so I turned away from him and stared at the wall.

'I must go now,' I said distinctly in a polite voice. 'Thank you so very much for calling.'

'Goodbye darling. See you on Wednesday. And Gloria . . . I love you.'

The receiver dropped from my hand as if it were a lump of lead. 'Who was that?' Morry asked as he walked past me down the hall, his hand on his chest.

'Oh, just some woman from my committee,' I mumbled. When he had shut himself in the lounge, I sat down on the telephone seat, and stared ahead of me blankly. Had I imagined it, or had Christian just said he loved me?

While I was preparing Morry's sandwiches, the telephone rang again. 'I'll get it!' I shouted, running into the hall and snatching up the receiver. 'Hallo?' I breathed.

'Gloria?' barked my mother's voice. 'What's this I hear about Sharon living with a Nigerian prince?'

Shocked out of the state of shock Christian's call had left me in, I quickly pulled myself together and decided to feign ignorance. 'Who told you that nonsense, Mummy?' I said with a laugh. Then, 'Don't tell me, it was Ruth, wasn't it?'

'Of course it was.' My head reeled under the betrayal: hadn't I asked her not to tell Mummy? 'Really, Gloria, why didn't you say anything to me?'

'I didn't want to upset you. Coming so soon after this business with Robert . . . Oh God, it's a tragedy,

Mummy, isn't it? I just don't understand what's happening to my children.'

'To my mind, there's only one tragedy around here, Gloria,' she snapped. 'That you've been walking round with your eyes closed to everything but housework all these years. Always on your hands and knees! Never sparing a thought for those children!'

'But I'm always thinking about them! Morry says I worry about them far too much – and so does Sharon and her . . .' I was about to mention Dr Kleinholtz, then stopped. (I don't know why I bothered really, since it seems there's nothing Angel doesn't know about already.) 'It's not my fault that they've kept things from me,' I continued.

'Well, you can't expect your children to be open with you if they see you keeping things from your own mother. It sets a bad example.'

'But I didn't keep anything from you. In fact . . .' My voice petered out. I mean, what's the use of arguing with Angel, when she always gets the better of me? Suddenly a wave of frustrated anger overcame me. 'How dare Ruth tell you, when she promised me she wouldn't!' I said.

'Just because you've been caught out, Gloria, don't take it out on your poor sister. We had dinner together last night – since no one in the family invited us. What were we supposed to talk about – the weather?'

'Hasn't Ruth got enough problems of her own to discuss? Must she talk about mine?'

'That's a very bitchy comment,' she said. 'It's not Ruth's fault that Mark has left her.'

'I suppose it's my fault that Sharon's living with a Nigerian, and that Robert is gay?'

'Sharon is a girl. You should have kept a closer eye on

her. As for Robert . . .' She sighed. 'I'm afraid he's just his grandfather's boy.'

What was she talking about? 'What do you mean, his grandfather's boy?' I laughed.

There was a long silence. Then, 'Surely you know perfectly well,' she muttered.

'Know what?'

There was another, even longer silence. 'About your father. About his ways.'

Suddenly I had an uncanny feeling that the floor was slipping away from under me. I sank down on the telephone seat and slumped against the wall. 'What ways?' I said.

She hesitated, and I had the rare feeling that for once she felt she'd said too much. 'His ways. You know. He . . .' She cleared her throat. 'Occasionally he . . . He had his flings.'

'Flings?' I repeated. 'You mean affairs?'

'Yes.'

'You mean,' I said carefully, 'that Daddy had affairs with women?'

She sucked in her breath. 'Not with women, no.'

Then . . .? Darling Daddy? My head spun. 'Oh my God!' I breathed.

'It wasn't very often,' she went on, her voice seeming to come from a great distance. 'Only from time to time. Times were different then, of course, it was illegal, one couldn't be open about it . . .' She cleared her throat again. 'Surely you suspected something, Gloria? I mean, why do you think he never minded that I had my admirers?'

Never before had these 'uncles' been alluded to – not since that night just after the war when Nanny had gone mad. 'I didn't know he didn't mind!' I said. 'I thought he must be hurt because you didn't like him!'

'I adored your father,' she said firmly. 'He was the most marvellous man.'

'Did you know about it?'

'Naturally.'

'But you stayed with him?'

'Of course I did. I loved him. We had one of the happiest of marriages.'

'But how can you say that when . . .'

'What he did in private was his own business, Gloria. I only minded if he was indiscreet, or put himself at risk. Like that night, the night that . . .' She stopped. 'How did we ever get on to this subject? Weren't we talking about Sharon?'

By now, however, my brain was working overtime, and I was back in the old Edgware house, with the acrid odour of smouldering carpet filling my nose. I had come in from a party, and the Fire Brigade was still there – yes, and the ambulance men who had come to take Nanny away. 'Like which night?' I insisted. 'Do you mean the night Nanny set fire to the house?'

'The woman was gaga,' Angel said in a strained voice. 'She would have flipped over anything.'

'But it wasn't anything, was it?' I whispered. 'Didn't she walk in on you and Uncle . . .?'

'Is that what you thought? Don't be ridiculous, Gloria! Of course it wasn't me!' She sniffed loudly, then blew her nose, and said, 'Now perhaps we can get back to the subject of your daughter. After all, the past is dead. What concerns me is Sharon's future. What are you going to do about it, that's what I want to know.'

Needless to say, as soon as Mummy hung up, I phoned Anne Green and put off our meeting indefinitely. How can I face her today, knowing what I've just found out?

The past is dead, Mummy said. That's what I used to

think, too – that it was a solid base one could stand on, and move towards the future from. Now, suddenly, that solid base is turning into shifting sand, and I'm losing my balance. Nothing is as I thought it was any more.

Thursday, 20th November

If the past is not as I thought it was, well, neither is the future turning out as I had intended it to. I am talking in particular about the immediate future, by which I mean the period this afternoon between one o'clock and three. That was when I had planned to spring-clean the house and start cooking Morry's dinner. Instead, instead . . .

Oh God, when Christian asked me to have lunch with him in his Clerkenwell flat, I should never have agreed! I had not planned to, had I? In fact, I'd only said I'd go to the pub with him after class last night to tell him why anything more between us could never be. So should I put the blame for my change of mind entirely on that second brandy? Or am I cursed with that same dangerous emotion I have often accused Sharon of having – a suicidal streak?

Did Morry notice my turmoil when I came home at a quarter-past eleven in the evening? He certainly seemed unusually sulky as, arms akimbo, he greeted me in the hall in his pyjamas with an angry, 'Where have you been?'

'Only at my writing class,' I said hurriedly.

He glanced at his watch. 'Till this hour of the night?'

That's when my bravado crumbled and I threw myself down on the telephone seat. 'All right, Morry,' I confessed. 'I've been drinking in a pub with a young man I'm in love with!'

He scowled. 'I'm in no mood for jokes, Gloria. I've been sitting here all by myself for hours. There was nothing worth watching on TV. What was I supposed to do – talk to myself?'

I stood up, shrugged my shoulders, and marched into the living-room. 'Well, you never talk to me. You've always got your nose buried in some novel or other.' I glanced with surprise at the tidy sofa and the sparkling coffee table, which was bare but for one folded-up newspaper. 'Where are all your books?'

'In the cupboard under the stairs, Gloria, where they belong.'

I frowned. 'But I didn't put them there this morning.'

'You don't have to tell me! I nearly broke my neck on one you left lying in the middle of the kitchen floor!'

'I left it there?' I gasped. 'I'm not the one around here who reads!'

'Neither, apparently, are you the one who does the housework any more!' he retorted. 'I've never known this house be such a bloody mess. Why, I've spent all evening clearing up – doing the dusting and Hoovering you used to do. I don't know what's got into you lately.'

I plonked myself down on the sofa, colour flooding my cheeks. 'I always thought you wanted to live in a pig-sty,' I remarked defensively. 'If I'm not as thorough about the housework as I used to be, I'd have thought you'd be pleased.'

He sat down on the other end of the sofa, and crossing his arms tightly over his chest, glared at me across the dust covers in hostile silence. 'A man likes a little company after a hard day's work at the office,' he said at last. That's when my guilty feelings caught up with me.

'Well, so how's business?' I mumbled. He began to speak, then stopped, and picked up the newspaper. 'Oh, for heaven's sake!' I exclaimed, losing my patience, 'What's wrong with you tonight?'

'Nothing,' he muttered from behind the headlines. Then, 'I don't feel well,' he grumbled. 'I've been having pains . . .'

I sighed. 'Where, this time?'

The newspaper lowered, and he pointed in the vague direction of his midriff. 'Here . . . and here.'

I narrowed my eyes. 'You've been eating hamburgers for lunch again, haven't you? Really, Morry, it's your own fault if you're feeling terrible. There's nothing wrong with you that a couple of Alka Seltzers wouldn't cure!'

And so we went to bed, and turned away from each other, as we've done every night for God knows how many years. Except last night, as I lay awake hugging my pillow, I wasn't remembering how things used to be between us, I could think only of today, and seeing Christian, and of how things might be.

I can't go to his flat, can I? The very idea of being unfaithful to Morry is disgusting.

Is it?

Of course it is. Especially after what Mummy told me about Daddy last week. Even setting aside the moral issues . . . Well, apart from anything else, with Sharon and Robert's lives in such turmoil – not to mention my poor sister facing financial disaster because she hasn't got any dresses left to sell – haven't I got a duty to be at home, in case I'm needed? Someone in this family has got to keep a hold on reality.

But wait a minute! I've just thought of something: if someone's got to remain on terra firma, why should it be me? Why shouldn't I enjoy going off the rails like they're all doing? Why, I deserve a little happiness too. That's settled it, then – I'm going to Clerkenwell. For once in their lives let the others look after themselves.

Later . . .

It is well past midnight. I am wide awake, restless. I ought to be tired after all that's happened since this morning. I ought to try and sleep. Yet I know I won't sleep if I go to bed. How could I sleep when . . .?

It's too late to start writing. And yet something has drawn me here, into Sharon's old room, to this desk. I look around at the flowered curtains, the old torn teddy bear sitting on the pillow, the candlewick spread, and nothing seems to have altered since I was here this morning. Yet, to me, it is as if a hundred years have passed. How can so much have happened? How can so much have changed? How can so much have been staring me in the face for so long and I never saw it? Oh, forgive me, my poor darling Morry!

The house is strangely quiet and comforting, almost as if the walls and the furniture know what is going on. The rooms have settled around us all evening like familiar, reassuring blankets. And yet there is an unreality about everything, an eerie emptiness here that nothing can fill. Someone is missing from the life of this house tonight, someone who is usually here.

All the events that have taken place since yesterday morning are swirling around in my head like clothes in a washing machine, tumbling chaotically in and out of vision. How to make sense of them? Where to begin? Where else but at the beginning, at the point where I left home, unaware that this was a day that would, in more than one way, change my life.

When I rode in the bus through the pouring rain towards Clerkenwell, there was only one thing I could think of – that I would be with Christian for the next few hours. However, despite my decision to go to his flat, I must have changed my mind a good forty times before I arrived there. Every red traffic light, every jam, every jerk of the bus seemed like an omen. 'Gloria, go back,' I told myself again and again. 'Go back to the safety of Hendon before it's too late.'

By the time I reached Clerkenwell my hands were clammy and my head was aching. As I walked up the dark staircase of the converted warehouse where he lives, my heart thumped with trepidation. But still I didn't turn back – no, I knocked on his door. He opened it almost immediately, and welcomed me with open arms which I fell into as gratefully as if I was coming home from an arduous trans-Siberian trek.

'I've only come to explain why I'm not staying,' I muttered as, pressing me close to him, he led me into a large open-plan living-room, bare but for a wall of bookshelves and two well-worn Victorian settees. He nodded, said that yes, he understood how I felt, why didn't I sit down and we would just talk a little.

The next thing I knew I was lying on a none-too-clean white fur rug beside a cast-iron stove, and he was leaning over me, kissing the inch or two of bare bosom that peeked through my unbuttoned blouse! Guilt and joy mingled together in my mind as I stroked his silver-streaked hair and contemplated what had just happened – that I, Gloria Gold, a 56-year-old housewife, had become an adulteress! No, those words sound far too cold to describe what had taken place. We had made love, that's what we had done, and with a passion, a tenderness and a natural pleasure I have never experienced with Morry – not even in the early days. Somehow, despite our newness to each other, it was all so easy and relaxed, as if we both already knew the other's body and its ways. As I lay there gazing at the flickering flames, it seemed to me that for the first time in my life I really understood why they say love-making makes two people one. Despite its being adultery, how right, not wrong, it seemed! All of a sudden I found myself thinking of Sharon, and wondering with a deep sadness whether being with Benedict felt at all similar for her, and if that was so, how difficult it would be for her to give him up to please me.

How dark and cosy it was in that large room, with the rain battering against the window-panes, and the traffic sloshing softly past outside, and the only extra light the flames of the fire. After a long silence Christian cleared his throat and said, 'What are you thinking?'

'Oh, this and that,' I said, somehow reluctant to tell him.

'I was just thinking how odd and yet how strangely natural it feels to be lying here in front of the fire with you,' he murmured as he traced a circle around my nipple. I swallowed hard, but said nothing. 'And that I would rather be here with you than with anyone,' he continued after a short pause.

A blush spread up my cheeks. 'Thank you,' I choked. 'I'm very flattered. I was thinking . . .' I hesitated. 'Well, that I had no idea "committing adultery" could be so wonderful.'

He laughed disbelievingly. 'Gloria, can it have taken you this long to find out?'

'You don't think I do this sort of thing every day?' I protested.

'Well, no, but . . .'

I shrugged him off, and covering my bosom up, heaved myself up on to my elbows. 'I'll have you know this is the first time I've ever done it,' I said with an embarrassed primness. 'In fact . . .' I stopped.

He rolled over on to his stomach, and frowned at me. 'Yes?'

My blush deepened. 'Well, you're the only man I've ever been with, except Morry.'

'You're kidding, Gloria.'

I turned my head away. 'I'm a different generation from you, Christian. I don't make jokes about such things.'

He sat up, pushed his flapping shirt-sleeves further up his arms, and hugged his bare knees. 'Well!' he said. 'Well . . .' He shook his head. 'In that case, I'm the one who should be flattered.'

'You?' I was about to protest, then changed my mind. A smile crept over my lips. 'Yes. Yes, you should,' I said with sudden pride.

He drew me close to him and kissed my face. 'Gloria, Gloria,' he whispered, putting an arm around my shoulder as he turned to gaze into the fire. How much tenderness there was in that voice! What a different expression from the one I've come to expect when Morry says my name! 'How strange that you should come into my life at this time, so that I could fall in love with you!'

My head spun, just as it did last week when he first said he loved me on the telephone. I looked up at his broad strong shoulders, his fine profile, his warm green eyes glinting red in the fire, and I thought to myself, Yes it's strange indeed that a handsome, talented man in his forties, a man who could surely have any woman he wanted, should fall for an old bag like myself!

'I can think of a million reasons why I like you,' I said. 'But how can you like me?'

'There's no "how" about it,' he said. 'I just do. There you are.'

Yes, there I was, half-naked on his fireside rug, a little late to contemplate the nature of his love, when all was

188

said and done. As I looked down at my semi-clad body and my creased, dishevelled clothes I thought suddenly of Ruth and of my mother and, again, of Sharon, and how shocked and surprised they would all be if they could see me there. And Morry? What would he think if he found out what his wife of thirty-six years' faithful standing had been doing that afternoon?

Ah, my darling Morry! Little did I know what you were going through! Little did I suspect how wrong I had been! But later, later. First let me write down what happened next:

'Besides,' Christian said as he stared into the fire. 'What makes you so sure you like me? For all you know I might be one big sham.'

'No, you're not.'

He lowered his head. 'The truth is that I am, Gloria. Believe me I am.'

I shivered. 'What are you saying? That you're a liar?'

'In a way,' he muttered from between hunched shoulders. 'You see, I've got to know you under false pretences.'

I moved away from him, and pulled my skirt down over my knees. 'I don't understand, Christian. Are you telling me your wife hasn't left you or something? Or that you don't love me after all?'

'Of course not, darling! No, it's nothing like that! It's just . . .' He took a deep breath and turned towards me. 'I told you once, didn't I, that Caroline left me because I didn't live up to her expectations? Well, I haven't lived up to my own expectations either. I . . . I lied to the class at the beginning of term when I pretended to be a writer of integrity.'

'Well, aren't you?' He shook his head. I shrugged. 'So what?'

He smiled sadly. 'I don't think you quite understand. I make you all look up to me because of the high literary standards I preach. But, you see, I don't practise them. I have no integrity at all any more. Oh, I did once. When I started out I wrote about things that were important, things that mattered to me. I tried to develop a literary style. It didn't get me very far. I've a whole drawerful of unpublished – and unpublishable – novels in my study and enough rejection slips to wallpaper a fair-sized house. So in the end, I sold out. Since then, I've achieved a modicum of success – but at the expense of my principles. Now I can't afford to have principles, because of my expenses.' He laughed at the irony. 'I write crap, Gloria. Cheap romances – not unlike Melanie Thatcher's, which is probably why I'm so hard on her. But real crap.'

'And it's published?'

He nodded grimly.

I put a hand on his thigh and said, 'I don't see anything to be ashamed of in that! Why, everyone has to earn a living, Christian. And if you can make a living by writing, I admire you for it, no matter what you write. Why, I know myself how hard it is to get more than half a dozen words down on paper. Now, to write a whole book – that's something to respect! Believe me, I'd admire you if you wrote the telephone directory.'

At this, his face broke into one of his wonderful smiles, and he threw back his head and laughed.

'Besides,' I went on, 'I've grown to like you because you're you – not because you have "literary integrity". Believe me, I couldn't care less about that.'

'Oh Gloria,' he said, embracing me. 'You are wonderful.'

'No, I'm not,' I said, pulling away from him again. 'In fact, I'm as big a liar as you are.'

he bloody six-mile limit. Might have known. Blimin'
Hendon. East, West or Central?'

'Just take me to Hendon. I don't care where.'

The traffic was terrible. We crawled forward inch by
inch. People strode past us – old men clasping walking
sticks and newspapers, career women in crisp smart suits,
and, as we approached Bloomsbury, young, laughing
students wound about with scarves which flapped like
flags in the wind. The taxi jerked forward, taking me
further away from Christian, the cabbie now accelerating,
now braking, all the time swearing under his breath.
To Southampton Row, where we were stuck behind a
belching lorry. Past the back of the British Museum –
once to me a depository of ancient dust, now the building
where Christian and I had first kissed – Good God, was
it only a week ago? My heart turned over. Oh Christian!
Whether anything more happened between us or not, he
would always have a special place in my heart.

Oh my God, I'm crying again, just like I was in the
back of the taxi – sobbing silently into a tissue, while the
driver glared at me in the driving mirror as if I was mad.
'You all right?' he said eventually, which was, when I
think about it, a very silly thing to say, seeing as I was
obviously not.

By the time we'd reached the Hampstead Road I was
being a little calmer. I'd dried my tears, and was reapply-
ing some make-up in my compact mirror. Well, Gloria
old, I told my red-eyed reflection, you're a lucky woman
to have a wonderful person like Christian fall for you, at
your age – more than that, to have him want you in 'that
way' too! To feel transports of passion you never felt in
old days with Morry, and to have those feelings
reciprocated – now, that's a rare thing at your time of
life, that's a real gift! And even though things could not

194

'Oh?'

'Yes,' I said. 'What makes you think you're the only
one with a well-kept secret? For all you know I may have
something weighing on my conscience, too. Tell me
something, why do you think I started coming to the
evening class?'

He pouted thoughtfully for a moment. 'I suppose,
ultimately, you came for the same reason most people do:
you wanted to be a writer yourself because of a love of
literature.'

I nodded with satisfaction. 'That's what I thought you'd
say. Well, you're wrong,' I confessed. 'I have no interest
at all in literature – whether you spell it with a big or a
little L. The truth is that I've been coming to your class
because I hate it.'

'What?' he said.

I nodded vehemently. 'I hate every writer that you care
to mention. You see, I hate all books.'

Then and there I told him the whole story: about
Morry's reading habits and how they had been annoying
me; of how Sharon had told me I needed a hobby; about
finding *Oy, Mother!* that fateful night back in September,
and deciding to get even with Daniel Z. Feigenbaum II.
As everything spilled out – even that shameful drunken
lunch with Claudia – it was as if a fog cleared in my mind,
and something I'd never seen before came clear to me.
'In a funny way,' I admitted, 'it wasn't the author of *Oy,
Mother!* I wanted to get even with, it was Morry and the
children. This whole business has been a way of justifying
myself.' Christian squeezed my hand, and I smiled wryly.
'Well, I haven't managed it,' I went on. 'I'm still a nagging
wife and a busy-body mother. Except now I know for a
fact that I'm not talented or clever –'

Here Christian interrupted me. 'But you are. Believe

191

me, you're far more intelligent than you realize, Gloria.'

I smiled. 'It's kind of you to say so, but I'm not. I'm nothing but an ordinary Jewish housewife who should have stuck to the two things she's good at – cooking and keeping the house clean.'

'You haven't got anything out of the class at all, then?' he said rather sadly. 'Funny, I always thought I was quite a good teacher.'

'Oh yes, I have got something out of it,' I insisted. 'My friendship with you. And that's something far more "creative" and valuable to me than any book.'

'Thank you,' he breathed, turning away from me, but not before I'd seen the tears in the corners of his eyes. 'So, my darling Gloria, where do we go from here?' he growled eventually, putting another lump of coal in the fire.

And where did we go? I wondered – and still do. Back to a student/teacher relationship in the classroom? Or forward to more illicit meetings in the British Museum? It's tempting, but . . . Face facts, Gloria. That Christian loves me I am now strangely sure. But how long will it be before that love disappears? I am fifty-six years old, he is a good ten years younger, and also on the rebound; in the prime of life, he has far to go. And me? Where am I heading? If I have learned anything during the last few months it is that there is no use pretending to be what I am not; and if I am not a writer, well, neither am I a 'professional' adulteress.

As I stared into the stove I saw Morry's face among the embers, and I realized that I could no more lie to him continually than I could any more to myself: though I had discovered in the past few months that my marriage was far from perfect, neither Morry nor I knew any other

existence; we were tied together by bonds any newly-forged ones could ever be.

Suddenly I knew where I had to go – Hendon, to make the best that I could of Abruptly saying I had to get back, I threw my clothes and, leaving a rather bewildere the top of the stairs, I ran tearfully out With the taste of his last kiss still sweet flagged down a taxi, and threw myself int

'Where to?' said the driver.

'Take me home,' I said. I gazed out th suddenly felt again – as acutely as if he w taxi next to me – the sensation of having around me, of feeling his body against n it before, and I realized that if we didn' each other I would never feel the warmt smell his particular smell again. Could shiver of regret passed down my spine a this bleak prospect.

There would be time to think over t For the present I had to get away. I bit n back my tears, and after a few mom the view through the window hadn't forward towards the driver and rap 'What's the matter?' I said. 'Why aren'

The bald patch in front of me pivote to a red-cheeked scowling face with a v

'Because, Madam,' he barked, 'yo where the hell to go. How am I suppo "home" is? For all I know, you cou Timbuctoo.'

'Hendon,' I muttered.

'Hendon,' he grumbled, pulling movement that threw me back in t

go on as they were with Christian – of this I was almost sure – I had learned something that might stand me in good stead: that people can, and do, behave in the most extraordinary way when they are in love; and I could be as easily swayed by my feelings as anyone else.

A surge of confidence welled up inside me as the taxi jerked onwards. I, Gloria Gold, was loved – not for my housework or for my cooking or for what I had or hadn't accomplished in my life, but better than that, I was loved for myself. Suddenly those anxieties about the children that are always at the back of my mind fell away, and I was overwhelmed by a feeling of power – as if I could do anything in the world I set my mind to. And that's when I had the idea to go and see Mark and Hattie, to try and talk sense into them.

I leaned forward and knocked on the glass, and the driver slid open the partition. 'I've changed my mind,' I said. 'I don't want to go to Hendon. Please take me to Mortimer Street in the West End.'

The bald patch swivelled on the thick red stalk of his neck. Incredulous lips opened. 'Mortimer Street?' he spat. 'That's in the opposite direction!'

'I know.'

'We've just come from there!'

'I know. I'm s –' On the point of apologizing, I stopped myself. After all, I was paying, wasn't I? He ought to be glad of a bigger fare.

'You've got to be fucking joking!' he shouted.

'No, I'm not fucking joking!' I shouted back. And then my mouth dropped open in shock, and, much to his surprise and mine, I burst out laughing: it was the first time I have used that swear-word in my life.

My surge of confidence lasted until I was standing outside the small second-floor showroom in Mortimer

Street where Mark and Hattie have temporarily set up shop since they've run off from Angel Dresses. What on earth was I doing here? I asked myself, as I climbed up the echoing stone staircase and hesitated outside the door of their showroom. I remembered suddenly my conversation with Angel the day Mark had left, when I'd said, 'Do you think I ought to have a word with him?' and she'd barked back, 'What good could you possibly do?' Well, what good could I do? I wondered now. What made me think I could succeed in talking sense into Mark when Ruth and Angel and Morry had failed? As Mummy had said, what authority did I have, and what did I really know about the business? At the time I'd agreed with her, I'd admitted that I knew nothing. But now I remembered what Christian had said to me before – 'You're far more intelligent than you realize, Gloria' – and, like a surge of adrenaline rushing to my head, the feeling of power came over me again. Of course I knew about the business! Hadn't I grown up with it all my life? Mummy was wrong when she said I couldn't do any good by talking to Mark – just as she'd been wrong throughout my life. A myth had arisen in the family that I was no good at anything; yet if Christian believed in me I must be more capable than anyone, myself included, had ever given me credit for.

I pressed the bell, and waited with a sick feeling in my stomach. Footsteps approached the door, the catch opened and Hattie was standing there, dressed in jeans and a loose shirt. Her welcoming smile (she must have been expecting a customer) died when she saw me, and her face, which at its best could be vivacious and pretty, took on a hard, set look nevertheless riddled with fear.

'Oh, hallo Gloria,' she said flatly, running her hand through her long blonde hair which, I noticed, wasn't thick and glossy as it usually was, but dull and lank, as if she hadn't bothered to wash it for a week.

'Hallo Hattie,' I said in a matter-of-fact way. She bit her lip and clutched the door with bone-white knuckles. 'Well,' I said eventually. 'May I come in?'

She glanced behind her unsurely, then back at me. 'What do you want?'

'I'd like to talk to my brother-in-law.'

She looked annoyed when I used the words. 'Mark's not here.'

'Oh?' I said. 'When will he be back?'

'I don't know. He's . . .'

Just then, I heard Mark's unmistakable jaunty step behind her, and his voice said, 'Who is it, darling?'

Hattie shot a meaningful look over her shoulder, but it was too late. 'Hallo Mark,' I called out loudly. 'It's me, Gloria.'

The door opened wider, and Mark appeared looking more than usually handsome. 'Gloria!' He smiled at me without embarrassment and, to my astonishment, kissed me on the cheek. I drew back. 'What are you doing here?' he asked genially.

'I want to talk to you,' I stuttered, taken aback by his ease.

'Well, don't just stand there,' he said. 'Come in, come in.'

He started to usher me inside, but Hattie put a hand on his arm to stop him. 'Mark, should we let her –?' she began.

Mark shrugged. 'There's no need to panic. It's only Gloria, darling.'

When I heard those words, it was as though a veil lifted, and I saw something about myself I had never seen before. Only Gloria? Wasn't that what I had always been

– to Nanny, to Mummy, to Claudia, to my husband, to Sharon and Robert – even to myself? Only Gloria, only a housewife and mother, only someone to service others, someone who didn't matter in her own right, someone who was never seen. But now I had been seen – I'd been seen by Christian – and to myself at least I'd never be 'only' Gloria again.

I looked contemptuously at Hattie, whose eyes slid away as if she didn't have the courage to face me, and I pushed past both of them into the showroom. That's when I had a further shock – when I sniffed the sour odour of fresh paint and saw the pretty decorations, the headed notepaper and the printed order-pads spread out on the matching wrought-iron tables and chairs. 'Hattie Styles' read the specially-designed logo. There was nothing temporary or quickly put-together about this showroom. So, leaving Angel Dresses had not been a spur-of-moment decision on their part – they had probably been planning their flight for months. And all the time, while this showroom must have been taking shape, Mark had been living with Ruth as if nothing was the matter between them, and Hattie had been taking the wages the company paid her every week! I sank down on one of the chairs, feeling dizzy, and stared at the rail of evening dresses in the corner, wondering how many of the samples were Ruth's best designs, and I asked myself if it had ever occurred to Mark that he had condemned not only Ruth to disaster, but also my mother, who had based her life around the business, and all the staff of Angel Dresses – the people who had worked faithfully for the family for years and years. I looked up at him coldly, and I could see by the benign smile on his face that no, of course he hadn't thought of them: on the contrary, he thought of no one but himself.

'How long has this been going on?' I muttered. Hattie looked at Mark and raised her eyebrows as if to say, I told you not to let her in, and Mark came and sat down beside me.

'That's irrelevant,' he said. 'What's done is done. And, believe me, it was high time.'

'Oh?' I said. 'Can you explain why?'

'Gloria, Angel Dresses has had its day. Yes, it did well for years, but now . . .' He sighed. 'Ruth and Angel don't seem to realize that times have changed since the business started. No one wants the sort of formal evening dresses Ruth makes any more.'

So in that case why did you take all her designs with you? I thought to myself. 'I see,' I said. 'So you think this is a proper way to make changes in a business? To run off with all the samples and leave Angel Dresses in the lurch – and at a time when money is crucial?'

He hesitated. 'If the company finances are in a mess, that's not my fault, Gloria, that's the recession. And believe me, if it hadn't been for me, the business would have folded many years ago.'

Oh yes? I thought, remembering how Mummy and Daddy welcomed him into Angel Dresses soon after he and Ruth were married, and how when Daddy died Mummy insisted that Mark take over the running of the place, even though he was never there – he was always off having lunch with someone or other, leaving Ruth to cope.

'And besides,' Hattie interrupted in a strained voice, 'I made most of those samples. I've a right to do what I want with them. I've got a right to have a fair share of the profits.'

I met her eyes. 'As a matter of fact, the company paid you well for your work, Hattie,' I said angrily. 'Those designs belong to the company, to Angel Dresses, not to you. And if you don't mind me saying so, I know for a fact that most of the dresses on that rail over there were designed by my sister. I'd recognize her style anywhere. They in no way belong to you.' Obviously she did mind me saying this, because her lips began to tremble. 'You'd have had more sense to stay put at Angel Dresses than to set up alone with Mark,' I went on addressing her, to Mark's evident surprise. 'You may manage to make a go of it this season by climbing on my sister's back. But when it comes to next season, I wonder what you'll do. Mark may have convinced you that he's the big "I am" at Angel Dresses, but believe me, it's Ruth who has always done the hard work. And how will you cope when you have to do all the designing without my sister to help you? She told me long ago your work isn't much good.'

At this she burst into tears and cried, 'Oh God! Oh, Mark, do something! How can you let her speak to me like this?'

Biting his lip, Mark went over and put a protective arm around her. 'There's no need to be rude to Hattie, Gloria,' he said in the uneasy tone which he always uses when he's trying to sound convincing.

'Can you give me one reason why I shouldn't be?' I retorted. Which made her cry even louder.

'Because . . . Because you're upsetting her.'

I shook my head. 'And why shouldn't I? She's stolen my sister's business, her husband and her designs . . .'

Hattie wailed louder, and Mark patted her on the back. 'Can't you understand?' he hissed. 'She can't cope with attacks like this. It takes her back to her childhood . . .'

I laughed shortly. 'Do you expect my sympathy? We all have our crosses to bear. For God's sake, Mark, forget all this nonsense and go back to Ruth! At least go back to the business and sort things out in a sensible way! Leave in a few months' time if you want to – but don't ruin the business too! After all, what's to stop you and Ruth getting divorced in a civilized fashion?'

'You don't understand,' he said desperately. 'I couldn't go back. This has all gone too far.'

Hattie broke away from him and, sobbing loudly, ran quickly out through a side-door, which slammed shut behind her – but not before I'd seen the swell under her shirt. I gasped. 'She's pregnant, isn't she?' I said to Mark.

Instead of admitting it, he turned on me furiously. 'Why don't you get the hell out of here, Gloria, and leave Hattie be? None of this has anything to do with you, you stupid fool! Damn you, you always had trouble minding your own business!'

And so saying, he followed her out of the room, leaving me alone. I stared blindly down at my hands, and forced back the tears that were welling up under my eyelids. So, my sister's marriage was really over, I thought as I listened to the sobs and comforting murmurings that were coming from the next-door room. Poor Ruth, I thought. And poor Angel Dresses! To have kept going for nearly sixty years only to be closed down like this! For from what Ruth had told me, I had no doubt but that 'Angel' would collapse without an excellent mid-season. And how could it have an excellent mid-season when all Ruth's best samples were now over here?

Over here. Right here, in the room with me. Hanging in front of me, within reach. Wiping away my tears, I stood up and went over to the dress-rail and fingered them lightly. Yes, this blue tafetta dress was unmistakably one of Ruth's gowns – and so was this red one – and this – and this – and this. Glancing at the door inside which Mark and Hattie had disappeared, I noticed to my amazement that there was a lock in it, and in that lock a key. I shook my head to try and shake some sense into it: no, I couldn't possibly! I told myself severely. I had always been such an honest person! Why, one of the first things that Nanny taught us was the commandment, Thou Shalt Not Steal. And yet I wouldn't be stealing, if I took them, would I? I would merely be returning stolen property to whom it belonged.

Nevertheless feeling like a criminal, I tiptoed over to the door and very carefully turned the key. The tiny click of the lock sounded like thunder to me, but it was thunder that neither Hattie nor Mark on the other side seemed to hear. That done, I grabbed my coat and handbag and, with fiercely beating heart, wheeled the dress-rail out through the showroom door and into the stairwell. It seemed like an hour till the lift came. Down, down, down it went. As I heaved the gates open on the ground floor, the silence of the building was interrupted by a yell and the dull distant thud of fists on a door. As I ran out into the wet street, dragging the heavy rail behind me, a window was flung open above me, and Mark leaned out, shaking his fist.

'What the hell do you think you're playing at, Gloria?' he yelled. 'Bring that rail back!'

'Come and get it!' I shouted as Hattie joined him in the window.

A torrent of foul abuse – far worse than anything I have ever heard Sharon use, even in her university days – rained down on my head from Hattie's lips. Ignoring it and the curious stares of passers-by as best I could, I struggled off, the dresses billowing out like great sails behind me. Round the corner into Great Portland Street I hurried, and thence into Margaret Street and the building which houses the Angel Dresses showroom. Another set of old-fashioned lift doors to be heaved open and closed, and then I was there.

'Gloria!' Ruth cried, jumping up from the desk as I burst in with a mixture of raindrops and excited tears streaming down my cheeks. 'Thank God you've arrived! Where have you been all day? I've been trying to find you for . . .' Her worried face went even whiter as I pulled the rail in after me. 'Christ,' she said in a stunned voice. 'What have you got there?'

'Don't you recognize it?' I said, catching my breath. 'It's your collection!'

She looked from me to the dresses incredulously, and then back at me again, and then she flung her arms around me and burst into tears. She cried for so long and with such fierceness that I was forced to extricate myself from her heaving embrace. 'Hold on,' I laughed, shaking her gently. 'I thought you'd be pleased. You're back in business, remember!'

'I am pleased, of course I am,' she insisted through her tears. 'It's just that . . .' She held me at arm's length, gripping my shoulders tightly, and at last looked me in the eyes.

When I saw her expression, my laughter died immediately. Suddenly I felt terrible. 'What's wrong?' I said.

'Oh Gloria, I've been trying to find you for hours,' she whispered. 'No one seemed to know where you were.'

'Tell me, quick, Ruth. What's the matter? Is it Mummy?'

She took a deep breath. 'No, darling. I'm afraid it's Morry. He was rushed to hospital at lunchtime.'

'I knew it!' I gasped. 'Those bloody hamburgers he's been eating! It's salmonella poisoning, isn't it?'

She shook her head and clasped me to her. 'I'm afraid

it's much worse than that, Gloria. He's had a heart attack.'

A heart attack. A heart attack. How many times have I heard those words used before, in relation to someone else's husband? 'He had a heart attack in his sleep.' Or, 'He dropped dead of a heart attack whilst mowing the lawn.' How many widows have I seen at weddings and barmitzvahs sitting at tables by themselves, putting a brave face on the fact that they're broken-hearted? And recently, at every function I've been to – we're getting to that age, I suppose – there's been a new face among them, and I've gone over and said, 'I'm sorry, Bessie or Hessie or whatever-your-name-is, I didn't know,' and they've said to me, 'It was terribly sudden. Thank God he didn't suffer. I suppose a heart attack's the best way to go.'

And now, out of the blue, it was my Morry who had had one, it was my husband about whom people might soon be saying those things. And there he was, grey as an unwashed sheet, lying in the Intensive Care unit of University College Hospital, with wires and tubes strapped to his chest and wrists. I stood outside the door supported by Robert and Sharon, staring in through the small glass panel, and it looked no more real than if I was watching a film. Yet that was my Morry in that high iron bed, and those were real nurses, not actresses, tending him. And those green lines on the electronic monitor did not rise and fall to some random pattern, they were tracing my Morry's life away.

What do you think at a time like this? You think, I never really showed him how much I loved him. You think, why did I nag him so much and make his life a misery, why didn't something tell me we were running out of time? And you think, it's too late to make up for it now, it's all over and done with. And then you think, what was I doing the moment it happened? How come I didn't know?

What had I been doing? I had been committing adultery. Yes, at the moment when my husband collapsed of a heart attack, I, Gloria Gold, had been making love with another man. The irony was that it had taken that for me to realize just how much my marriage mattered to me, and this was something my husband could never know.

'Can I go in and see him?' I whispered to the young doctor who was standing beside us.

'Of course you can, Mrs Gold,' he said. 'Robert and Sharon have already been in. But only for a moment, please. It's important that he's not overtired.'

I nodded, and began to push open the door, then stopped as I remembered the joke book which had started me off writing all those months ago: 'Why do Jewish husbands die young? Because they want to.' Surely not? I thought. I turned back. 'He's going to live, Doctor, isn't he?' I asked.

His smile was hesitant. 'From what we can tell, the prognosis looks good at the moment,' he said. 'It appears that the heart muscles are relatively undamaged. If that's so, we might well be able to do a by-pass operation. The surgeon will be making that decision in about an hour.'

I felt faint for a moment, and then became aware that Sharon was squeezing my hand. 'Are you all right, Mum?' she said.

'Of course.'

'Do you want me to come in with you?'

I noticed the doctor exchange glances with Robert, then he said, 'I think it's better if your mother sees your father alone.'

So, he's critical, I thought. Keeping my emotions under

control, I left all three of them at the door, crossed the floor and sat down on the chair beside his bed. I reached for his hand, and when I felt his fingers cold in mine, I could hold back the tears no more. 'Oh, Morry!' I wept, bending low and kissing his knuckles. 'Oh, my darling Morry! What will I do without you?'

'Hold your horses, Gloria,' came a slow, croaky voice from the pillow. 'I'm not dead yet.'

I sat up with shock: I hadn't known he was conscious. 'Morry!' I said. 'Thank God you're awake!' I wanted to say –'

He smiled weakly. 'Don't get so excited, doll,' he whispered, forcing out the words with difficulty. 'With all these pretty nurses about, I don't want you lying in the next bed.'

I gave him a watery smile. 'Oh, Morry,' I sobbed. 'Do you know how much I love you?'

'Do you, Gloria?'

'Of course I do.'

'I love you too.'

He turned away, and seemed to drop off to sleep for a moment while I sat there beside him, holding his hand. Then he came to with a start and said, 'I'm sorry . . .'

'What for?'

He gave a tiny shrug. 'For causing everyone so much trouble.'

'Morry,' I said, 'how can you apologize for such a thing? It's not your fault you're ill. You –'

He raised his other hand as if to silence me. 'My business . . .' he muttered.

'Morry, this is no time to talk about dresses!'

He shook his head weakly, and tears welled up in his eyes. 'It's gone, Gloria.'

'What do you mean?'

nothing I could do, and that I'd not be allowed to see him till later this morning because they were afraid of me, Gloria Gold, bringing germs into Intensive Care.

A by-pass. To me, it sounds like part of the North Circular Road. And it all became necessary because I gave him too much chicken fat? Suddenly the Chosen diet is fatal? What has God been playing at for the past four thousand years?

I wonder what Christian is doing now? It's strange to think he has no idea what terrible things have been happening. I wonder if he's thought about me since I left him? I wonder if he really cares?

I mustn't think about him.

I have just phoned the hospital, and the night-nurse said Morry is sleeping peacefully.

I think I'll turn in now. Good-night, my darling, good-night.

Epilogue

The house is spotless, the dining-room table is laid with my best china, there's a fresh bar of soap in the downstairs cloakroom and a chicken casserole simmering on top of the stove with Morry watching over it. I can smell it from here – it's filling the house with a wonderful aroma. I've an entire free hour before the family arrives for supper so I've come up to Sharon's old room, to write a sort of farewell message to myself. Just sitting down at this desk makes me feel rather queasy – I haven't sat here since the night of Morry's operation. And as I'm starting work soon after Christmas I don't think I'll ever have time to write my autobiography again.

Yes, I, Gloria Gold, have got a job. I made a resolution to get one last night, while I was watching *Dynasty*. What with Morry's business having closed and the next month or so devoted to his convalescence, we're going to need some money coming in.

'You don't have to go out to work,' Morry said when I told him my decision this morning. I looked up from the kitchen sink to the chair where he was sitting, his hair almost white, his cheeks pitifully pinched, his frail body wrapped up in the new woollen dressing-gown Robert gave him as a get-well present, and I smiled. 'I know I don't have to, Morry.'

'Well then, forget it,' he said. 'I'm sure it won't be necessary. I'll be well enough to work again in a few weeks' time, and I'll manage to set something up. If the worst comes to the worst I'm sure I can get a job in someone else's business. We can live on our savings till then.'

'We could,' I said. 'But it wouldn't be sensible. Because in the meantime our savings will all disappear.'

He hung his head. 'I'm sure the children would help out if we were short.'

'They've already volunteered to help, when you were in hospital. And I said no. We don't need their money. They work hard enough for it, they deserve to enjoy it themselves.'

He sighed. 'Gloria, I know what you think of working women. You don't have to become one.'

'But I want to, Morry,' I insisted as I yanked the plug out of the sink. 'It's time for me to make my contribution. After all, you've kept me for the last thirty-six years. If I can earn a few pennies to keep us going through this difficult time, well, I'll be delighted. And if we find we can manage without my wages when you're back at work – why, then I'll stop working, or if I'm enjoying it I'll spend the money on myself.'

Tears came into his eyes, as they have done many times since his open-heart operation. 'You're a wonderful woman, Gloria,' he said. 'Do you know, I never saw quite how wonderful you were until now.'

'That's because you never looked further than those bloody books,' I said briskly, hoping he wouldn't notice the tears that were pricking my eyes. 'Besides, I'm not wonderful,' I added, overcome with guilt as I thought

213

suddenly of Christian. 'I'm just an ordinary wife, doing what any wife would do when her husband's just had a major operation.'

'Well, I think you're wonderful anyhow. But are you sure you know what you're letting yourself in for?' he added. 'I mean, it might not be easy to find a job at all – for a woman of your age, with no work experience . . .'

I rounded on him, invalid or not. 'What do you mean, no work experience?' I shouted. 'What do you think I've been doing every day for the last thirty-six years?'

At noon I dressed myself up in my best clothes and, trying not to look too nervous, set off for an employment agency that I've often passed in Golders Green. As it turned out, I never arrived there. Because on my way past the shops, I bumped into Angel.

'Gloria dear!' she exclaimed as she caught sight of me. (All my life I've been 'you' to her. Now, since I brought the collection back from Mark and Hattie, suddenly I'm 'dear'.) Her gaze swept over me, starting at my leather boots and finishing at the new purple silk scarf which was a 'cheering-up' present from Sharon. 'Mmm,' she grunted, eyeing it approvingly. 'I like that colour. I think I'll get myself one of those. But where are you off to dressed so smartly? Why aren't you at home looking after your husband?'

'I'm going to get a job,' I said. 'I've decided I ought to be earning till Morry gets back on his feet.'

'A job? About time too, if you don't mind me saying so,' she said. 'It won't hurt you to work for a while.' Then the tip of her nose crinkled doubtfully. 'It's very virtuous of you to want to help out, but there are over three million people unemployed, you know. What sort of job do you think you'll be able to get? After all, you've never done anything.'

My confidence sank. 'Well,' I faltered. 'I'm sure I'll find something. Remember, Mummy, I trained as a secretary.'

'In 1950!' she said tersely. 'Oh well, since you've waited thirty-six years to look for a job, I don't suppose it'll matter if you wait a few minutes longer. Let's go and have lunch.'

'Well, actually . . .' I hesitated. I had promised Morry that I'd be back soon, and the last thing I needed before going to the employment agency was forty minutes in my mother's company. I was about to say no, but then a funny thing happened: as I looked at Angel standing there on the pavement, I suddenly saw her with new eyes. The bright mask of make-up on her face; her smart coat in the latest style; her sheer, black seamed stockings; her puffy feet crammed into those ridiculous high-heeled shoes; rather than these things hiding her age as she hoped they did, I realized that they only made it more apparent, and I saw her for what she was – a 79-year-old woman who was afraid of losing her last charms, just as once upon a time she had probably been afraid of losing Daddy. She won't always be here to have lunch with, I thought to myself. And then I remembered the day Sharon and I went to see Dr Kleinholtz, and how hurt I'd been when she'd refused to come out afterwards for a bite to eat. Then it occurred to me that, for all Angel pretends that she's so awfully busy, when it comes down to it she's probably rather lonely since she retired. That's why she calls me up every day, I realized, that's why she's always asking me to do things for her, to take her somewhere or to pick her up. 'I'd love to have lunch with you, Mummy,' I said, suddenly feeling flooded with affection for her.

She gave me a suspicious look, as if she'd guessed what I'd been thinking. 'Don't do me any favours,' she grumbled. 'I'm not at the age where you have to humour me yet.'

I smiled to myself and took her arm, and together we walked down the road to Maxi's, her favourite coffee house. But when we went inside, I nearly turned right round and walked out again. Because never in my life have I seen such a mess. Mountains of dirty crockery were piled up on the tables, and there were crumbs and scrunched-up napkins all over the unswept floor. Half a dozen customers were clamouring to give their orders, as many again were calling for their bills, and the two young, harassed waitresses ran hither and thither without any method, taking orders here, spilling drinks there, tripping in and out of the kitchen with empty trays when the tables were crying out to be cleared.

'What a mess!' I couldn't help but exclaim.

Angel shot me an angry glance as she marched over to her favourite table, which was snowed under with used plates. 'For heaven's sake, Gloria, just sit down. I promise you won't be poisoned.'

'I'm sorry, but can't we go somewhere else?' I asked. 'I just won't enjoy being in here. It's disgusting. What on earth has happened to Maxi's? It never used to be like this! Why, what it needs is a good wash-down and a bit of organization!'

'I know,' said a voice behind me. 'But you try finding decent staff.'

I turned around to see a woman of about my own age and build, looking glumly at me from under a head of heavily-lacquered strawberry-pink hair. With that mental Masonic handshake I once told Christian about, we both realized that the other was Jewish, and her face relaxed into a friendly smile. 'I'm Maxine,' she said, holding out a plump scrubbed hand to me. 'I'm the owner of this joint.'

'How do you do?' I said, quite taken aback. 'I'm Gloria Gold.'

'And you're Angel's daughter? I've seen you two together in here before. Oh yes, I know your mother well. Angel's been coming here for years, haven't you, darling?'

My mother turned on one of her most charming smiles. 'Hallo Maxine dear. You'll have to forgive what my daughter says. I'm afraid she's obsessed with hygiene.'

'Mummy!'

But Maxine laughed, and her worried blue eyes twinkled. 'Oh! I could do with someone like you here,' she confided. 'My old manager retired a fortnight ago, and the replacement I hired was so hopeless I had to get rid of her straight away. I'm on the till myself, and I'm lost without someone capable. I'm doing my best but you know what it's like – I've only got one pair of hands. And try finding a reliable person who's willing to serve and organize a kitchen!' She shook her head. 'I'm giving up hope of finding someone with enough experience.'

And then the idea struck me like a bolt of lightning. 'What do you call enough experience?' I said. 'How about thirty-six years?'

Life is a strange thing, isn't it? You plan to do something, and you get distracted from it, and you end up doing something else. Who would have thought that when Mummy asked me to have a coffee with her this morning it would lead to me becoming a restaurant manageress?

'A common waitress!' Angel grunted with disapproval after I'd agreed terms with Maxine. 'Right here in the heart of Golders Green. In Maxi's, where I come with all my friends! Couldn't you have found yourself a better job somewhere else? After all, you did train as a secretary.'

'As you reminded me before, that was a long time ago, Mummy,' I said. 'Besides, kitchens are what I know and love best.'

Dr Kleinholtz says that it's high time I stood up to Angel. 'It seems to me that she's always destroying your confidence,' he said during the last of the three private sessions I've so far had with him. 'You are locked into a mother–child pattern of behaviour that should have ended when you were an adolescent.'

'Well, it didn't,' I told him. 'And it's far too late to do anything about it now.'

Dr Kleinholtz, however, insists that it isn't, and that our relationship could change just as mine with Sharon is doing, with a little re-education of *the mother without* as he refers to Angel, and also of *the mother within*.

'That makes it sound like I've swallowed her,' I remarked. Which, despite his usual po-face, made him laugh quite a bit.

'That is a good analogy,' he said. 'For in a way that is exactly what has happened: you have ingested her ideas. Her fears have become yours; her insecurities your insecurities. So ideas pass from generation to generation, unless one breaks the pattern.'

Which is, I suppose, what Sharon did all those years ago when she moved to Kentish Town. Though it still smarts to think that she kept her address a secret from me for so long, I'm beginning to understand why she did. Will things be different when she has a daughter of her own, I wonder? If she ever has one? Oh, God, will I ever have a grandchild? I can't bear to think of my poor baby being childless for ever!

I must stop this. As Dr Kleinholtz says, Sharon must decide what she wants for herself. I only hope she decides she wants a baby eventually, because I really couldn't bear it if she didn't have one, even though Dr Kleinholtz says that's only because I'm afraid of my own mortality . . . Damn it, psychotherapists don't know everything, do they? Doesn't he have any family feelings? Surely even someone as clever as he is can't explain instinct away?

Oh well, if there's one thing I've learned since Sharon persuaded me to go back and see him by myself, it's that there's no point worrying about these things. Because for all the nagging I did in the past, Sharon is still living in sin with Benedict, and for all my praying he was heterosexual, Robert is still, as he calls it, gay. And things could be worse, couldn't they? As it turns out, Benedict is a quite remarkable person, with delightful old-fashioned manners even Nanny would have approved of. And Robert is living with a nice Jewish heart specialist who not only makes the best egg-and-onion I've ever tasted, but also helped save my husband's life.

So what do I really have to worry about – that is, as long as they all stay healthy? I know that the doctors say Morry – touch wood – is on the road to recovery, but what about the boys? Though I try not to think about it, I do sometimes lie awake some nights, worrying about their futures . . . Dr Kleinholtz agrees that AIDS is one of my real, as opposed to my 'neurotic', worries. I'm afraid it's only too real – you can't open a newspaper without reading about it nowadays.

I'm only glad that Robert has settled down, and with such a fine person as Peter. Really, no daughter-in-law could cook such lovely meals for my son as he does when he's home from the hospital. As for Sharon – well, though any girl can marry a lawyer or an accountant, it takes someone special to bring home a real live prince. Besides, as Dr Kleinholtz often points out, whether I approve or disapprove of what she does, it doesn't actually make the slightest difference, because she'll carry on doing it anyhow.

If you can't beat them, join them, I suppose. Which is why I've succumbed to Morry's wishes and taken the hall druggets up at long last, and why the whole lot of them are coming round for a low-fat Friday-night meal this evening: Sharon and Benedict, Ruth and Mummy, Robert and Peter – oh, yes, Anne and Harry Green, Peter's parents, too. I'll never forget the way they turned up to see Morry at the hospital with a basket of fruit and a bunch of flowers . . .

What will the conversation be like tonight with all of them sitting around the table? One thing is certain – it's bound to be lively, and Morry could do with a little cheering up. I've never known him so down in the dumps as he's been since that operation. Maybe it's the thought of being out of work that's making him so depressed. If so, there's a marvellous surprise in store for him – Ruth told me on the phone this morning that she wants him to join Angel Dresses in Mark's place.

Oh, how I'm looking forward to having all the people I love round my dining-room table!

All except one of them.

I wonder what he'll be eating for supper? I wonder if he's alone? I wonder if he's looking forward as much as I am to our meeting next week?

'I'm only coming round for half an hour,' I insisted when he last telephoned me.

'Yes, darling.'

'Because I'll have to get home, to look after Morry.'

'Mmm,' he breathed.

'I won't be able to stay. We'll just talk, won't we?'

220

'Whatever you say, Gloria,' he laughed softly. 'Your wish is my command.'

What a man! Is it my fault I can't resist the temptation of seeing him this once more – if only to say a proper goodbye? Thank heavens there'll be no time for any hanky-panky to happen between us because, frankly, I've really missed his kisses over the last few weeks. Well, maybe there will be a little time . . .

God knows, love is too precious a thing to throw away when you find it. And life is both too short and too exciting to spend the whole of it scrubbing things clean. And what Morry doesn't know can't hurt him, can it?

Can it? I'll have to ask Dr Kleinholtz.

That is, if I can ever summon enough courage to tell him about my affair with Christian.

Sharon was right all those months ago when she told me I needed a hobby. I may not have learned much about creative writing, but I have certainly learned a lot about me. First, that I am only human. Second, that . . .

Oh, blast, there goes the doorbell. I've got to . . . Heavens, what's that smell of burning? Oh my God, I completely forgot the casserole! But wasn't Morry supposed to be keeping an eye on it?

Morry!